STRIKE THREE!

STEPHEN D. SMITH with LISE CALDWELL

Standard®
PUBLISHING
Bringing The Word to Life

Cincinnati, Ohio

From Stephen

For my in-laws—Betty and Hank. Thanks for
telling everyone about these books. And thanks
to Jenny Willig for all of the technical stuff!

From Lise

For Shan, my darling husband.

Text © 2006 Stephen Smith and Lise Caldwell. © 2006 Standard Publishing, Cincinnati,
Ohio. A division of Standex International Corporation. All rights reserved. Printed in the
United States of America. Project editors: Greg Holder, Lynn Lusby Pratt. Cover and
interior design: Rule29.

ISBN 0-7847-1729-X

12 11 10 09 08 07 06   9 8 7 6 5 4 3 2 1

Library of Congress Cataloging-in-Publication Data

Smith, Stephen D. (Stephen Dodd), 1961-
  Strike three / Stephen D. Smith with Lise Caldwell.
      p. cm.
  Summary: As she is getting ready to graduate from eighth grade, Stephanie relies on
God's help when she joins a softball team with some angry teammates, makes a new friend
who is struggling with anorexia, and tries to figure out her changing relationship with the
boy who has been her best friend since grade school.
  ISBN 0-7847-1729-X (pbk.)
  [1. Christian life--Fiction. 2. Softball--Fiction. 3. Anorexia nervosa--Fiction. 4.
Interpersonal relations--Fiction. 5. Competition (Psychology)--Fiction. 6. People with
disabilities--Fiction.] I. Caldwell, Lise, 1974- II. Title.

PZ7.S659382Str 2006
[Fic]--dc22

2005032091

CHAPTER:01

Stephanie stayed underwater as long as she could. She loved the feeling of holding her breath until she thought her lungs would explode.

What she wasn't counting on was a wall of water in her face when she broke the surface. She gasped, inhaling the chlorinated water, and coughed. When she could finally breathe, she pounced on the culprit.

"Todd," she sputtered, grabbing her older brother and giving him a knuckle noogie on the head.

They both laughed as she clung to him, until Todd lost his grip on the balance bar and slipped under the surface. Stephanie Swift's laughter abruptly stopped as she pulled him back up.

"Gotcha again," he grinned. But the pinched look on his face assured her that he hadn't been kidding.

"OK, you two, knock it off," Todd's red-haired physical therapist said. "We have work to do. Stephanie, let's take Todd for a walk."

"Yes, Sergeant Hollingsworth!" Stephanie said, saluting—anything to make Todd crack a smile.

"You know, Rhonda," Todd said, "we could just drown her now and put her out of my misery!"

"To do that," Stephanie said, "you'll have to catch me."

"Deal." Todd looked grimly determined.

"Let's see what you've got, Todd." Rhonda looked visibly relieved that the splash fight had ended. "Your parents are paying big bucks for your therapy."

"Wait a minute. You get paid for this?" Todd asked, pretending to be shocked. "I thought you did this because you cared!"

"Yeah, yeah." Stephanie grinned and slicked back her long dark-blonde hair. "I'm getting paid too, you know. Dad said I get 1 percent extra of our inheritance for each session. Pretty soon, it will all be mine, mine, *mine!*"

Todd laughed. "You call Dad's collection of Mr. Potato Heads an inheritance?"

Stephanie nodded. "You should see what they're worth on eBay!"

Stephanie wouldn't have given up this time with Todd for anything. She'd been his most constant companion since the car accident almost a year ago that had left him unable to walk. He had been out one morning picking up a small refrigerator for his college dorm room when a speeding driver, talking on her cell phone, ran through a stoplight and smashed into Todd's car.

At first, doctors told Stephanie's mom and dad that their son would never walk again, but after just two months of therapy, Todd wiggled three toes on one of his feet. Six months later, he could bend his knees slightly. That's when the rehabilitative therapy started. Stephanie promised God that if he would spare her brother, she would do anything and everything possible to help him heal.

"OK, Todd," Rhonda said, "your sister will support you on the other side. I've got you on this side. But I want you to hold onto the bars with your hands and see if you can support your body weight with your legs. We need to strengthen your lower back muscles."

"She means your back end!" Stephanie laughed.

She swam over to her brother's side, planted her feet on the pool bottom, and steadied Todd's back in case he started to fall. She prayed this would be the day Todd's legs decided to work again—the day he would jump out of the pool, grab a towel, and try to snap her with it. But the reality was that if Todd could just support himself and move one leg forward, it would be a good day.

"Be patient, Toddy," Stephanie whispered into his ear so that only he could hear.

Todd swayed back and forth and then stilled himself. Stephanie felt his right bicep relax. Her brother was letting off the pressure from his arms. A huge smile crossed his face.

"I'm doing it," Todd said excitedly. "I'm standing, and I can feel the pressure on my legs."

"You're kidding," Stephanie said with equal enthusiasm. "Seriously?"

"Seriously, Steph," he replied.

"Excellent!" Rhonda said. "Now concentrate on the other side of the pool. Focus."

Rhonda coolly commanded Todd to take a step. Stephanie worked hard to remain calm, but her breath grew shallow as she watched Todd take one step and then another and then another. She glanced up to see her mom with her face pressed against the pool's glass enclosure, watching her son take his first steps in more than a year. Even Rhonda, who usually remained professional, grew wide-eyed. But Todd wasn't paying attention to any of them. He was focusing all of his energy on taking as many steps as possible.

"Look at the other side of the pool, Toddy," Stephanie whispered to her brother. "Keep your eyes on the prize."

Todd managed to shuffle about four feet across the therapy pool before wobbling and falling. Stephanie and Rhonda caught him.

"Would you mind if I just swam a lap or two?" Todd asked. Stephanie could see the exhaustion in his eyes. "I don't think I can walk anymore."

"Sure, Todd," Rhonda said, "but let me spot you so you don't drag your feet along the bottom."

"OK," Todd agreed, "this time. One day I'll be swimming on my own."

Stephanie pulled herself out of the pool and dangled her long, tanned legs in the water.

"I'll just stay here and call you names," she taunted, her green eyes dancing with joy.

She rarely got angry with her college-age brother, but they teased one another mercilessly. Everyone said you could tell they were both Swift kids, not only by their blonde hair and green eyes but also because of their identical sense of humor.

"Sounds good, little sister," Todd said, "but remember, turnabout's fair play."

Stephanie looked around their kitchen. The celebration was in full swing, and if she hadn't known better, she would have thought it was Christmas and the Fourth of July all rolled up in one. Her mom was dishing up all of Todd's favorite foods—pot roast with carrots and onions, mashed potatoes, apple pie, and homemade yeast rolls. Her grandmother, not to be outdone, was decorating an elaborately frosted cake.

Stephanie's dad was recording it all on the video camera, and Todd was playing one of his favorite CDs. Stephanie was setting the table, which had been her dinnertime chore since she was six. It still seemed strange to set a place where there was no chair. Todd would just roll up in his wheelchair when dinner was served.

"Come on, Grams," Todd said, "the cake looks beautiful. Let's eat. Some of us worked up an appetite in the pool this afternoon." He winked at Stephanie.

"OK, mister," his mom said, "be patient. This is your celebration."

"Yeah, but I don't want to miss it because I've passed out from hunger," Todd replied, grabbing a steaming roll out of the basket.

"Sandy," Stephanie's dad said, turning to her mom, "say a little something into the camera."

Mom turned toward him. "A little something into the camera." Then she waved it away with a dish towel.

Stephanie finished setting the table, her own stomach growling, and helped her dad carry the food. Finally, they all gathered around the table. All of them, except Todd, remained standing and held hands.

"Todd, would you like to say the blessing?" his dad asked.

"Absolutely," Todd replied. "Lord, I want to thank

you for the steps you allowed me to take today. I want to thank you for my family. If you feel another flood might be needed, I ask that it be about waist high so I can walk everywhere. I want to thank you for letting Grams be here this weekend. Be with Gramps so he doesn't burn down the house trying to cook while Grams is gone. Lord, be with Steph tomorrow at softball tryouts. And finally, Lord, thank you for this food. I ask that you use it to nourish us and strengthen us for tomorrow's challenges. You are an awesome God! Amen."

"Amen," everyone echoed.

"Why can't we eat like this every night, Mom?" Stephanie asked.

"Because we'd all be fat as pigs," she said. "Pass the rolls, dear."

Stephanie watched her grandmother grind pepper over her food—even the rolls. Her plate was almost black with pepper.

"Careful, Grams," Stephanie said, grinning. "Be sure to save some pepper for your apple pie!"

Grams pinched her cheek. "The doctor said pepper makes you live longer."

"Then you may outlive all of us," Todd told her.

"How's school going, dear?" Grams said, turning to Todd. "Is that community college campus wheelchair accessible?"

"Oh yeah, Grams," Todd replied as he passed the gravy to Stephanie, "it is, but my school's been out for three weeks already. Unlike other kids at the table who still have two weeks left. But I doubt I'll need the ramps much longer. Isn't that right, sis?"

"Totally," Stephanie said, looking up from the gravy to her grandmother. "You should have seen him today, Grams. He walked halfway across the pool!"

"That's wonderful, Todd," Grams said absently, as she watched her granddaughter pour gravy over her food, "but you shouldn't build yourself up for a letdown. Stephanie, don't you think that's a lot of gravy?"

Suddenly, the room got quiet. Stephanie loved her grandmother, but she sure had a knack for sucking the joy out of any situation. Stephanie set down the gravy boat, tried to take a bite, and then put her fork back on her plate. She noticed Todd vigorously stirring his iced tea, the grin that had been on his face all afternoon wiped away.

Stephanie wanted to say something to Grams— wanted to tell her not to take away Todd's hope—but she caught her mother's eye first. Mom shook her head no ever so slightly, so Stephanie kept her mouth shut. The remainder of the meal, which had been such a celebration, was remarkably quiet.

Stephanie picked at her food. She felt like her

grandmother was watching every bite she took. Stephanie had never worried about her weight. She played sports and swam and ate what she wanted. Did Grams notice something different about her?

As soon as they could, Todd and Stephanie excused themselves and retreated to the family's back deck. The Illinois days warmed up nicely, but as the sun went down at night, the air reverted to its cool springtime crispness. Stephanie and Todd often sat on the deck reading, doing homework, or just talking. Tonight the deck was not only a welcome escape from Grams, whose allergies made her avoid the night air, but Stephanie knew that Todd was eager to talk about what had happened that day—and to pray about it.

Jesus had become a big part of their conversations since Todd's accident. The Swift family had always attended church, but Todd and Stephanie had both thought youth group was pretty lame before.

Stephanie's first reaction after the accident was to yell at God. As she looked out through the pine trees toward the sunset, she remembered that time when Todd lay injured in the hospital. So many people from their church had come to see them, talk to them, and pray with them. Pastor Jeff had even brought Chinese takeout when Stephanie had complained about how many meals she had eaten in the hospital cafeteria.

One afternoon, while Todd underwent more

surgery, Pastor Jeff's wife Carrie came and sat with Stephanie and her parents. After a few quiet moments, Carrie had asked, "Stephanie, do you want to go for a walk?"

Stephanie was thrilled to escape the boredom of the waiting room. She and the pastor's wife took the elevator down to the first level and walked out into a courtyard filled with large oak trees and lots of ivy and lavender.

"You want to sit awhile?"

"Sure," Stephanie said, shrugging her shoulders.

They sat down on a stone bench. Stephanie really wanted to act grown-up and mature, but she felt totally awkward holding a conversation with this woman who was practically a stranger. Stephanie nervously picked at a piece of lint on her sleeve.

"This must be really hard for you," Carrie said.

Stephanie hated when adults said that. What did they know? And how was she supposed to respond to such an obvious statement?

"Yeah," Stephanie grunted.

They sat quietly for several long moments. Finally, Stephanie couldn't take the silence anymore. She started to say something, but stopped when she saw tears oozing out of Carrie's eyes.

"What's wrong?" Stephanie asked, surprised by this display of emotion.

"Sorry," Carrie said, wiping her face. "It's just that being here with you makes me remember."

"Remember what?"

"Being at the hospital. Waiting during treatments. Wondering what was going to happen. See, when I was about your age, my younger sister was diagnosed with leukemia."

"Wow!" said Stephanie. "How is she now?"

"She died, but I know that in Heaven God has given her a new, healthy body, and that someday I'll see her again."

"Oh."

Carrie's words jolted Stephanie to her core. That moment had been the first time Stephanie acknowledged that Todd could die.

Todd's voice startled Stephanie out of her reverie. "Come back, sis. Where did you go?"

"I was just thinking about my talk with Carrie in the courtyard that day. I don't even remember everything she said, but I know it was the first time I wanted to take Jesus seriously—to really find out more about him. I was baptized about a week later."

Todd sighed. "I'm not glad that the accident happened, and of course, I would change things if I could. But I'm really grateful God used it to draw you and me closer to him."

"And to each other," Stephanie said, resting her head on Todd's shoulder. "You're the best big brother in the whole world."

"I know," he said, grinning.

She sat up and punched him in the arm.

"Watch it," he said. "You're trying out for softball tomorrow, not boxing. By the way, are you nervous?"

"I'm OK," Stephanie said. "I'm not sure if I'll make pitcher. I doubt I'll be the best one there. But I hope I can at least play first base. It's not as much fun to sit on the bench."

"You'll be fine," Todd reassured her.

"It's only a game anyway," she said.

"Good attitude. Do your best, and whatever is meant to happen, will happen."

"Let's just hope I'm meant to at least play first base." Stephanie stretched. "I think I may head on up to bed. You did great today. You'll be walking on dry land before you know it."

"Maybe," he replied.

"Don't let what Grams said get you down."

"Right back at ya. 'Night, Steph."

"'Night, Toddy."

CHAPTER:02

The alarm sounded at eight o'clock. Stephanie reached over and smacked the top of her Astroboy alarm clock. Her dad had gotten it for her when he went to Japan on business when she was eight. It was a little figure of a boy with pointy black hair, standing next to a robot with a clock in its stomach.

Astroboy was one of her dad's favorite cartoon characters. Her dad loved all kinds of collectible stuff—*Star Wars* figures, old lunch boxes, and of course, his Mr. Potato Heads. Growing up, Stephanie thought it was normal. When she realized that no one else's dad had a basement room set up like a scene from *Lord of the Rings*, she was a little embarrassed at first. But now she just thought it was totally cool. He was still a kid at heart.

Stephanie lay in bed on her back, staring at the ceiling. Most Saturday mornings she enjoyed sleeping late, but softball tryouts were on her agenda today.

She said a quick prayer to calm her already jittery stomach and rolled out of bed.

Stephanie paused in front of her mirror on the way to the shower. She lifted up her T-shirt and examined her stomach. Why had Grams made such a big deal about the gravy? Stephanie had the first hint of curves, but her mother said that was totally normal.

Sighing, she slapped her tummy and shook her head. For years Grams had made hurtful comments to her mom, and Stephanie had seen how much it hurt her mother. She didn't want to stress out about everything like that. She decided not to worry about her grandmother. Grams would be going back home to Iowa the next day anyway.

After dressing, Stephanie went downstairs to grab a quick breakfast before leaving.

"Hey, Mom," Stephanie said, kissing her mom on the cheek.

"Morning, sweetheart. Did you sleep well?"

"Like a baby," Stephanie replied, pouring herself a glass of orange juice.

"Oh, did you suck your thumb, itty-bitty babykins?" Todd asked, rolling into the room behind Stephanie.

"No," Stephanie teased, "but I drooled a lot."

Stephanie and Todd both laughed, but their mother just shook her head.

"Watch it, you two. Don't let your grandmother hear you talking that way."

"Why not?" Todd asked. "She doesn't seem to worry too much about what she says in front of us."

Stephanie glanced from Todd to her mother. She never had the nerve to talk to her mom about Grams. But Todd always went straight to the point.

"Your grandmother shouldn't have spoken to you the way she did last night. You know your father and I have total confidence that you'll walk again."

"Me too," Stephanie added, sipping her juice.

"Aren't you having anything else for breakfast?" her mom asked. "This isn't about what Grams said to you last night, is it?"

Stephanie saw her mom and Todd glance at each other, but chose to ignore it.

"I'm not anorexic, if that's what you're worried about," she said, grabbing a banana. "I'm just too nervous to eat much this morning."

Stephanie's dad dropped her off at the ball field where tryouts for the Chapel Hill Saints, a ponytail league for the Chapel Hill park district, were being held. Last year Stephanie had played in the bobtail middle school league, but now as a graduating eighth grader, she was eligible for the high-school-aged ponytail league of fast-pitch softball. Or at least for the freshmen-only team.

Stephanie grabbed her glove and cap and pushed on the car door just enough for it to close. Her dad rolled down the passenger side window.

"Have fun," he said. "Use the Force."

"Thanks, Yoda," she replied, laughing, and walked around to the driver's side to kiss her dad's cheek. Her dad saw the *Star Wars* movies as an allegory for God's spiritual battle of good versus evil.

A group of girls passing by stared. The blond in the middle mumbled something like, "*Star Wars* is for losers," and the girls around her giggled. Stephanie and her dad ignored them.

"You have your cell phone?" her dad asked.

"Got it, Dad. I'll call when we're finished."

"See you soon," he said, and drove the Volvo out of the parking lot.

The field was already crowded with groups of girls, whispering or tossing softballs back and forth. A few sat on bleachers. Stephanie noticed the blond girl and her giggling friends sitting on the pitcher's mound.

Stephanie made her way through a small group and headed up to the bleachers along the first-base line. One beautiful girl, her curly chestnut-colored hair falling over one eye, sat alone at the top. She wore an oversize T-shirt and capri pants. But even so, Stephanie thought she could be a model or an actress or something.

"Hi," Stephanie said, trying to sound friendly, "I'm Stephanie Swift."

The girl looked surprised at being spoken to, but replied, "Alexis Wilson."

"You here for tryouts?" Stephanie asked, knowing as soon as she'd said it that it was a lame question.

"Yeah. You are too, I guess," she added, sounding neither surprised nor happy.

"Do you mind if I sit with you?" Stephanie asked.

"No," Alexis said, "please."

After sitting quietly for a few moments, Stephanie asked, "So . . . did you grow up around here?"

"No, my family just moved here from Dubuque, Iowa. My dad got a job with the Illinois Department of Agriculture."

"Do you know where you're going to high school yet?" Stephanie asked.

"East," Alexis said.

"Hey," Stephanie said excitedly, "me too!"

"Cool." Alexis's smile revealed perfect teeth.

Stephanie wondered if tryouts would ever get underway. All the coaches were over there, but they seemed too busy checking out their charts and lists to start. Stephanie noticed the rude blond girl and her friends move over to the second set of bleachers.

"Oh, I don't know," Stephanie heard the blond say. "I'm probably not really the best pitcher." She laughed when she said it and flipped her hair over her shoulder.

"Are you kidding, Jackie?" a girl on her right said. "You were the best player on our bobtail team. You know you're going to be fantastic."

"OK, you're right," Jackie said. "I just hope the coach agrees." She giggled again. "If not, though, my dad will talk to him. He's the owner of Wolfe Electronics, you know. He's the one who paid for the team uniforms."

Oh great, Stephanie thought. *She's Jackie Wolfe.* She'd heard stories about this girl and how she always managed to get exactly what she wanted. Stephanie wasn't thrilled that she and Jackie were going to be on the same team. Stephanie turned to Alexis.

"So what are you into besides softball?" Stephanie asked Alexis.

"Not much really," Alexis said. "Sometimes I do some modeling."

Stephanie noticed Alexis looked a little embarrassed about it.

"Really?" Stephanie asked. "That's great. You

know, when I first saw you I thought you looked like a model."

"Thanks," Alexis said with a shrug. "I'm really getting too fat for the camera."

Stephanie glanced at Alexis. It was a little hard to tell underneath the baggy clothing, but Stephanie was pretty sure Alexis was the thinnest girl she'd ever seen. She didn't really know what to say.

"So . . . is it fun to be a model?" she asked.

"Yeah, I guess, but it's a lot of work. The only good thing about it is that my parents have been putting most of the money away in my college fund. I guess there's almost enough in there now for all four years."

"Wow!" Stephanie said. "I bet your parents are thrilled."

She thought of her own dad. A few weeks ago she'd found him late one night sitting at the kitchen table looking at financial statements. He didn't want to talk about it, but Stephanie knew that Todd's medical bills and therapy were being paid for out of what was supposed to be her college fund. She didn't mind. It made her feel like she was helping. But still, she wondered how she'd pay for college when the time came.

"My dad thinks it's time I stopped, or at least slowed down," Alexis said. "Sometimes I have a hard time keeping up at school when I have to travel. But my mom is really pushing me to model all summer. I'd rather play softball."

"What position do you play?" Stephanie asked, hoping she wouldn't say pitcher.

"Pitcher," Alexis said. "You?"

"Pitcher or first base."

Stephanie saw Jackie turn around and stare at both of them. When she caught Jackie's eye, Jackie's mouth smiled, but her eyes narrowed. She turned back around and whispered again to the girls sitting around her, who once again burst into giggles. A few of them sneaked looks at Stephanie and Alexis.

"Want to go warm up our pitching arms?" Stephanie was ready to escape Jackie's hive.

"Sure."

When they got to the bottom of the bleachers, Jackie walked over to them.

"Hi," she said, in a surprisingly sweet voice. "I'm Jackie Wolfe. And you are?"

"Stephanie Swift."

"Alexis Wilson."

"Nice to meet you," Jackie said. "I'm sure it'll be terrific playing on the same team together. But would you mind if I gave you a little piece of advice?"

Stephanie wasn't in the mood for whatever game

Jackie was playing, but Alexis seemed to think Jackie was being sincere.

"Sure, that'd be great," Alexis said.

"OK, here it is. Don't bother trying out for pitcher. I know for sure that position has already been filled." Jackie stared hard at Alexis.

"Filled?" Stephanie asked. "By whom?"

"By me, of course," Jackie said, her voice not so sweet this time.

Stephanie felt the silver cross resting at her throat. It was a constant reminder of who she was now in Christ. It took all of her self-control not to tell Jackie Wolfe exactly what she thought of her.

"I was under the impression, Jackie," Stephanie said in a voice equally sweet, "that positions were determined *after* tryouts—not before."

"I was just giving you some friendly advice," Jackie said, but this time all the sweetness was gone.

"Wow!" Stephanie said sarcastically. "Thanks."

Jackie glared at Stephanie for a moment and then turned and walked back to her buzzing hive. Alexis looked a little shaken.

"Maybe this wasn't such a good idea," she said. "I think I'll call my dad and have him pick me up."

"You'll do no such thing," Stephanie said. "Don't let Jackie get to you."

Just then the head coach blew his whistle. "Listen

up! Everybody take a seat on the bleachers. Let's get this thing started."

Coach Terry Becker was a slim man, a few inches shy of six feet. His hair was turning gray, but he had bold blue eyes, a big smile, and a dimple in his chin. He wore a pair of khaki shorts and a team T-shirt. When he turned around to hurry up a few stragglers, Stephanie saw the Wolfe Electronics logo on his back.

Next to Coach Becker stood a young woman in her early twenties. Her name, Stephanie would soon learn, was Jennifer. She was the assistant coach and trainer for the Chapel Hill Saints. Her light-blond hair and pale blue eyes were a sharp contrast to her golden tan.

"I want to thank you ladies for getting out of bed this morning," the coach joked. "Let me reassure you that you're not trying out today for a place on the team. All of you will make the team, but Jennifer and I need to evaluate your skills so we can assign positions and determine the lineup. Now, before we begin—"

Jackie raised her right hand and waved it dramatically. Coach Becker at first seemed intent on ignoring her, but since she was sitting directly in front of him, it was impossible.

"Yes?" he asked, looking irritated.

"I was just wondering if you really meant that all of us had to try out for positions," Jackie said.

"I believe I meant exactly what I said," Coach Becker replied gruffly.

"It's just that since I had the best record in bobtail for no-hitters, I figured I should be the pitcher. I don't think I really need to demonstrate anything. I think my dad may have talked to you about—"

This time it was Coach Becker's turn to interrupt. "You must be Miss Wolfe. I have, in fact, had several conversations with your father, and I've been quite clear with him. Each of you must earn her position on the field and in the lineup, not only by your performance but also by your attitude."

He looked directly at Jackie while he said this, but she just smiled a knowing smile and flipped her long blond hair over her shoulder.

"I want a winning team, but that isn't my number one goal," Coach Becker continued. "My goal is to help each of you develop your skills. There will be plenty of time to showcase your abilities in your junior and senior years when the college talent scouts start coming around. Right now, on my team, everyone gets to play."

Coach Becker sent them out to the field. As he walked away, Stephanie saw Jackie roll her eyes behind his back.

"What is wrong with her?" Stephanie muttered.

"I guess we're about to see how good she is," Alexis replied.

Coach Becker and Jennifer began assigning girls to different positions, and each of them walked around among the girls, making notes. At one point, Alexis, Jackie, and Stephanie were grouped together for pitching. But Stephanie realized Coach Becker's method was unlike any she had ever experienced. The coach lined up the three girls parallel to one another, and when he blew his whistle, they were all to throw at the same time.

"Have you ever pitched like this before?" Stephanie whispered to Alexis.

"Never," Alexis replied. "Good luck."

"You too," Stephanie said. She turned to Jackie and decided to be nice. "Good luck."

"I don't need luck," Jackie replied.

Stephanie concentrated on her target markers in the batter's box set forty feet away, just like on a real baseball diamond. She couldn't tell much about what Jackie or Alexis was doing, but she heard Coach Becker instruct Jackie more than once to keep her eyes on the batter's box, not the other girls pitching.

Stephanie loved to fast-pitch, because the stance reminded her of bowling. She held the ball in her hand, raised it over her head, took a step back, and then wound her arm in a windmill, letting go of the ball as her arm was on the upswing. Just before the ball snapped out of her hand, she pivoted her hip.

Stephanie's previous coach always told her she had good form and accuracy, but her speed was too slow. And the next phase of the tryouts involved a speed gauge. The girls relaxed for a moment as Coach Becker prepared. Stephanie said a silent prayer, asking for wisdom.

"Nice job," she told Jackie.

"Thanks, I know."

OK, thought Stephanie, *I guess that's how you're going to be.* She turned instead to Alexis.

"You have great form, and your speed is really good," Stephanie said. "How do you pack that kind of muscle power being so thin?"

"Thanks!" Alexis blushed. "I wish I *was* thin!"

Stephanie figured Alexis had been around models so long she had a warped view of thinness. But she didn't have much time to think about it, because Coach Becker was ready to measure their speed.

CHAPTER:03

"Hey, Steph," Stephanie heard a voice say, "you looking forward to the roster tonight?"

Stephanie looked up from her biology book to see Heather Fleming and Amanda Gordon, two of the girls who were at tryouts. Although they went to the same school, Stephanie never remembered either of them speaking to her before. She closed her book, marking her place in it, and sat it on the ground next to her.

"Oh, hey," she said to them, hiding her surprise. "Yeah, it'll be interesting. I'd kinda hoped to pitch, but with Jackie and Alexis around, my best shot is as relief. But that's OK."

"So do you think Jackie Wolfe will be the pitcher?" Amanda asked.

"Probably," Stephanie said, remembering now that Amanda had been one of the giggling girls with Jackie before tryouts. "She's really good."

"Well," Heather said, "see you at practice tonight." Heather glanced behind Stephanie and smiled. "Oh hi, Matt!" Then she and Amanda hurried away, giggling.

"Yeah, see ya," Stephanie said. She looked up at her friend Matt. "Hey, Matty, when did you get so tall?"

"Growth has been a lifelong project of mine," the dark-haired, brown-eyed Matt said, plopping down next to her. "What's up with those two?"

"What do you mean?" she asked.

"You know. Why are they suddenly so chatty?"

"They were at softball tryouts yesterday," she replied. "They were just being friendly."

"They were just checking out the competition."

"Matthew Ford," Stephanie replied, "you're such a cynic."

"If you expect the worst from people," he said, "they never disappoint you."

Stephanie elbowed him in the ribs. "You know you don't really feel that way."

"Not about you, at least." He grinned mischievously.

Stephanie and Matt had been friends since fourth grade, when she had accidentally destroyed his meticulously recreated model of the solar system by overestimating the amount of baking soda needed for her science-fair volcano. By the time she finished helping him put his project back together, they were fast friends.

In fact, Matty was really her only good friend at school. She hung out with kids from all different groups—the softball girls, of course, and the smart kids in her classes. Until this year she'd played flute, so she knew most of the band kids too. But mostly she found that she didn't have much in common with them, especially since Todd's accident. Stephanie realized she just took life a little more seriously now than most of the other kids.

But Matt had stuck by her after Todd's accident. He'd really been a good listener when Stephanie needed to talk. She didn't know what she would have done without him. Sometimes she wondered what would happen when she and Matt started high school in the fall. He played football, and she figured she'd hardly ever see him once the season started. Besides, lately things had felt a little weird between them. Stephanie knew that tons of girls had crushes on Matt, and most people thought she was going out with him. But they were, and always had been, only friends. Stephanie just hoped it could stay that way.

She glanced at Matt, wondering if he would push the Amanda and Heather issue. He didn't. Unwrapping his roast beef sandwich, he took a big bite and told her about a book he'd just finished reading. As they got up to go to their next classes, he grabbed her elbow.

"Stephy," he said, "I don't trust those girls."

"By 'those girls,' you mean Amanda and Heather?"

"Yeah, I don't want to see you get hurt," he said, looking more serious than usual.

"That's sweet, Matty," she said, "but don't worry. I'll be fine."

Although the sun had sunk low in the sky, the air was still thick and muggy on the ball field that evening. The girls started showing up at Chapel Hill Park at six-thirty, even though Coach Becker had made it clear he wouldn't arrive until seven. Stephanie had told herself it was silly to be nervous—ridiculous to come early. She was already on the team, after all, and even these initial lineups would most likely change as the season progressed. So she was irritated with herself when she couldn't eat anything at dinner that night and took her dad up on the offer to go a few minutes early to practice. When she got there, it looked like the rest of the team had already arrived. She said hello to several of them, including Heather and Amanda, and made her way to Alexis, who sat on the bleachers in the same spot.

"You nervous?" Stephanie asked, noting Alexis's pale face and trembling fingers.

"A little," she said. "Mostly just cold though."

Stephanie looked at her in surprise. How could anyone be cold on a warm night like this? Alexis looked a little embarrassed, so she didn't push the issue. Instead, Stephanie glanced around the field. The girls mostly stood in groups of two or three.

"I don't see Jackie anywhere," Stephanie said.

"She's not here yet," Alexis replied.

Stephanie was a little surprised. She had expected Jackie to be there before anyone else. But before she had time to wonder any more about it, her thoughts were interrupted by the revving of an engine. She looked up to see a white convertible BMW screeching into the parking lot. Jackie Wolfe rode in the passenger's seat, and a man Stephanie assumed was Jackie's dad was at the wheel. Jackie looked a little like an old Hollywood movie star from the 1950s, wearing big sunglasses. A silk scarf held her hair in place. She pulled off both the scarf and the glasses, said good-bye to her dad, and strolled leisurely across the parking lot to the ball field.

Heather and Amanda shrieked and ran across the field to meet Jackie, jumping up and down and pointing at the convertible as it drove off. Jackie obviously loved the attention. Stephanie remembered Matt's words and decided she might not relate this to him. She was afraid to prove him right and further destroy his faith in humanity.

Moments later, Coach Becker arrived, and all the girls made their way to the bleachers. Stephanie practically had to pull Alexis down to one of the lower places.

"Ladies," Coach said with authority as he waved the roster in the air, "this piece of paper is a list and that's all. The names in the starting positions are simply those whom I felt were stronger than others—maybe just a little stronger, maybe a great deal stronger. Things can change. The starters on this list may not be starting in three weeks."

Stephanie looked around at the other girls. Some looked afraid, while others looked impatient. She could understand both emotions. Even she, who normally didn't let things like this get to her, wondered what the coach had in store for her. She was certain Jackie would be the starting pitcher, with Alexis as relief. But Stephanie would gladly take first base or any other position on the field.

"So here's the deal," the coach continued. "I'm going to post the sheet now. Jennifer and I need to meet with a few of the other coaches, so we'll start practice in fifteen minutes. But starting Wednesday, practice will be a solid two hours with no break. Bring your water bottles."

Coach Becker walked over to the fence that protected the spectators from the batter and fastened the roster to a clipboard attached to a post. As he walked away, some of the girls in the front row raced to check it out. Stephanie and Alexis rose and followed the stream of girls crowded around the roster. Suddenly, Stephanie heard a loud obscenity. A moment later, an angry Jackie pushed between her and Alexis, marching directly toward Coach Becker.

"Wow," Alexis whispered to Stephanie, "I guess she's not starting."

"No, she's not," Stephanie said as she read the names on the roster. "You are!"

"No way!" Alexis said. "Seriously?"

"Seriously," Stephanie said. "Congratulations!"

"Thanks, but I think Jackie is going to hate me. What are you playing? Can you see?"

"Yeah," Stephanie said as she squinted, "looks like left field. Huh. I've never played left field before, unless you count first-grade kickball."

As the girls continued to chatter about the postings, Stephanie and Alexis walked back up the bleachers to gather their gear. When they paused at the top and looked down, Stephanie saw Jackie waiting impatiently for Coach Becker to stop talking to his assistants. Intrigued by what would happen next, the girls sat down to observe, as did several others. Finally, the coach turned around to confront Jackie.

"Excuse me, Coach Becker," Jackie said, "you made a mistake on the roster."

"I doubt that," Coach Becker replied coolly. "What do you think is wrong?"

"I'm not the starting pitcher. I thought I made it clear at tryouts that my father—"

"And I thought I made it clear, Miss Wolfe," Coach Becker said, interrupting her, "that I am the coach of this team and will make my decisions without regard to who is financing the uniforms. If you wish to remain on this team, I suggest you accept that. Is there anything else?" His voice was cool, but his eyes snapped with anger.

Stephanie thought surely Jackie would back down, but, evidently, Jackie had more nerve than Stephanie imagined. Jackie's voice still had the fake, overly sweet tone that Stephanie was growing accustomed to.

"I'm sure you'll change your mind," Jackie said. "I *am* the best pitcher in the league, and I'm the only person on this team who deserves to be the starting pitcher."

The whole team stared open-mouthed at the confrontation between Jackie and the coach. Coach Becker gazed down at Jackie.

"You're right. I may change my mind and let Stephanie pitch relief instead if you do not return to the bleachers this instant. I will not tolerate these willful displays of disrespect." Jackie, amazingly, opened her mouth to say something else, but Coach Becker cut her off. "That will be all, Miss Wolfe. Please return to the bleachers."

Jackie tossed her hair and pivoted on her right heel to march away.

"Wow!" said Alexis. "She's brave."

"No," said Stephanie, "just spoiled. I think she's got some plan to get her dad to force Coach Becker to let her pitch."

Jackie returned to the bleachers and was immediately surrounded by her beehive of girls. Amanda tried to put her arm around Jackie, but Jackie shrugged it off. Stephanie couldn't hear her next words, but all the girls in the group laughed, and a few glanced up at Stephanie and Alexis.

"That can't be good," Stephanie said, smiling slightly. "I think now they're going to hate us both."

Honestly, she didn't really care what girls like Heather and Amanda thought of her, and Jackie certainly wasn't someone she wanted as a friend. But still, it wasn't going to be much fun to be on a team with girls like that.

"Why do they even want to hang around her?" Alexis wondered.

"Probably hoping to get a ride in that convertible," Stephanie said, retying her shoe. "I mean, Jackie's pretty and popular. Even if she is—" Stephanie hesitated. She and Todd had talked a lot about only saying things that would build people up and not tear them down.

Alexis finished the sentence for her, "—a conniving little snake, you mean?"

Stephanie laughed. How could she argue with that?

A few moments later, Coach Becker returned. He smiled at the group and seemed determined to move past his conversation with Jackie.

"You have all now had a chance to look at the roster. I think there may have been some surprises. A few of you are playing positions you've never held before. Miss Swift, for instance," he said, looking at Stephanie, "is playing outfield. You've never done that before, have you?"

"No, Coach," she said. "I kind of wondered about it."

"You have a really solid throwing arm, and your aim is great. You don't quite have the speed to be a starting pitcher, but I feel confident you'll do well in a position that demands distance and accuracy."

"Cool," Stephanie said with a smile. "Thanks, Coach!"

Another girl raised her hand. Stephanie recognized her from school. Her name was Natalie, a slender girl with short blond hair. She looked more like a cheerleader than a softball player, but she had been an awesome second baseman on Stephanie's bobtail team last year.

"Coach, I'm a little nervous about playing catcher," Natalie said. "I'm used to second base. Don't get me wrong. I'd love to learn something new."

"We'll go over all of the positions and rules as we begin our practices," Coach Becker said. "I chose you for catcher because you obviously catch the ball well, and your height makes you a good candidate to play behind the batter's box."

"Do I need to buy my own gear?" Natalie asked.

"No," the coach assured her, "the team has gear for you to wear."

Heather raised her hand. Stephanie shifted nervously. What would she say?

"I just want to say that I think you should let Jackie pitch. We all know she's better than the other girl. I won't play unless Jackie is starter."

The girls let out a collective gasp. Even Jackie turned quickly to look at Heather. *She must be really desperate for Jackie's friendship*, Stephanie thought.

"OK," Coach Becker said as he scanned another copy of the roster. "Jenny Frost, you are now starting at first base. Next question."

Heather started to speak, but the coach cut her off.

"Here's the deal, ladies," he said. "You are all thirteen and fourteen years old. You have not coached softball. You were not promised a specific spot in the lineup. I, on the other hand, am as old as your parents, maybe older. I have coached softball. Jennifer here was one of the girls on a team I coached ten years ago. Now she's out of college and coaching her own high school team next spring. We do want this to be a great experience for you, and we want you to have a great time. But not a single one of you is more deserving of a spot than any other. Miss Fleming here just gave up a starting position thinking I would buckle under pressure. Sorry, Heather, that won't work with me.

"We'll begin our first practice by actually playing a game. For those of you who are playing a position for the first time, do your best and make a mental note of your relevant questions."

The coach divided all of the girls into two groups of nine players each, plus three rotating players. He then instructed one group to take the field in the positions they were assigned.

Alexis stood on the pitcher's mound. Stephanie sat on the bench with Jackie, Heather, and Amanda.

Terrific, Stephanie thought. *My own little fan club.* But she smiled as she sat down with them, hoping they could get past the earlier confrontation. She took a seat near Heather and was amazed when Heather, along with the other two girls, moved to the opposite end of the bench.

Stephanie normally wasn't hurt by the stupid behavior of others, but this snub forced her to take a deep breath to fight back the burning sensation of unshed tears. She focused on the game and prayed that Alexis, who looked quite nervous out on the mound, would do well.

The first up to bat was a girl named Kelsie. Stephanie had never seen her before, except at tryouts. Kelsie took her place in the batter's box and prepared for the pitch. Alexis stood on the pitcher's mound, rolled her arms around backward like a windmill to warm up, and then straightened up. She placed one foot in front of the other, braced her feet, and gripped the ball. With a rapid jerk, she backed up while at the same time spinning her arm up over her head and down behind her. As the ball passed her thigh and went forward, she pushed into the pitch, sending the ball at top speed across the forty feet between her and the batter. The ball slammed into Natalie's glove.

"Strike one," Jennifer called.

Two more pitches like that sent Kelsie to the

bench. Heather was up next, but was so noticeably upset that she struck out immediately without much effort. Amanda, on the other hand, put up a fight. By the time her second strike was called, she had three balls. The last pitch would be the deal breaker. If Alexis pitched a strike, she would have completed a no-hitter inning. If the pitch went slightly wrong, it would send Amanda to first base on a walk.

Stephanie felt a bit guilty because she was silently rooting for Alexis and not for the girl up to bat from her own team. Alexis released the ball. Stephanie held her breath as Amanda swung and missed.

"Awesome," Coach Becker clapped. "Great job, Alexis! A no-hitter inning your first time up. Good for you!"

A beautiful, sunny smile spread across Alexis's face, revealing why she was such a successful model. Alexis approached the bench along with the other girls playing on her practice team.

But as Alexis began to walk past Jackie, Jackie blocked her path. "Is it really true that you're a model?" Jackie asked, in that sweet voice Stephanie had already learned meant Jackie was up to something.

"I do some modeling, yes," Alexis said, blushing.

"What kind?" Jackie asked, her smile wide, her eyes fixed on Alexis.

"Oh, catalogs, print ads—" Alexis began.

But Jackie interrupted her. "No, I mean regular or plus-size?" Heather, who stood nearby, snickered. "It's just that you seem a little, well, large to be a model." Jackie smiled maliciously, and her friends cackled. Stephanie would have slapped her if she could have gotten near enough. But it was just as well she couldn't, because she would have regretted it later.

Alexis's face went pale. Fortunately, she didn't have to say anything because Jackie and her swarm headed for the outfield. Stephanie, who should have followed them, stood transfixed. She had no idea what to say to Alexis. Jackie's words had been so cruel—and so ludicrous—but she was afraid Alexis wouldn't believe any of her reassurances.

"Will you be joining us, Miss Swift?" Jennifer asked impatiently. Stephanie gave Alexis a quick hug and then ran toward left field, glaring at Jackie as she passed the pitcher's mound.

Stephanie watched as Jackie threw her first pitch. The girl who was up to bat, Mollie Larson, took a lucky swing and sent the ball into right field. The right fielder, Elise Wagner, missed the ball but ran after it and got it to first base just after Mollie was called safe. Stephanie could see the furious look on Jackie's face and felt guilty, again, to be rooting against her own teammate.

Next Jackie pitched to Chrissie Rose, who made solid contact with the ball on the second pitch and sent it into left field. Stephanie easily caught it and threw the ball to Amanda at second base, who tagged out Mollie. The rest of the practice went fairly smoothly.

"I'm exhausted," Alexis confessed to Stephanie as they walked to the parking lot together.

Stephanie wasn't tired at all, but she didn't want to make Alexis feel bad. She looked up and waved at Todd waiting in the minivan. Todd waved back.

"Who's that?" Alexis asked. "He's cute."

"That's my brother Todd," Stephanie answered.

"Wow! Why don't you invite me over sometime?" Alexis asked, laughing.

"Sure!" Stephanie replied.

Alexis looked embarrassed. "I was just kidding. I mean, I don't want to just invite myself over or anything."

"No, I think that would be great. Hey, why don't you come over on Saturday after practice? We can hang out all day—maybe go to the pool or something."

"That would be awesome," Alexis said.

Todd honked the horn, and Stephanie ran toward the van, waving back at Alexis.

CHAPTER:04

"How was practice?" Todd asked, as Stephanie climbed into the van. The van had been customized so that Todd could control the gas and brakes with his hands instead of his feet. It also had a lift for his wheelchair. Stephanie's mom had been terrified when he started driving again. After all, he'd gotten his injuries in a car accident in the first place, but Todd loved the freedom it gave him.

"Practice was, um—" Stephanie realized she was about to say "good," but it wouldn't be the truth. The previous week Pastor Jeff had preached on being truthful in everything and not allowing your conversation to be filled with little white lies.

"Yes?" Todd asked.

"Practice was not great actually. One of the girls, Jackie, was really unhappy that she wasn't made starting pitcher. She made a big scene with Coach Becker and said some nasty things about one of the other girls."

"Who?"

"Alexis, the one I walked out to the parking lot with," Stephanie replied.

"She's really pretty," Todd observed.

"A little young for you, don't you think?" Stephanie said, grinning.

Todd laughed. "*Definitely* too young. But I mean she looks like she could be a model or something."

"Actually, she is. But I think she's pretty insecure."

"They usually are."

"But isn't that weird?" Stephanie asked. "I mean, to be one of the most beautiful people anyone knows and to be insecure?"

"Think about it," Todd said. "The rest of us get to have good days and bad days, but her job is to be pretty all the time. If she doesn't look the way some photographer thinks she should, she's fired."

"I never thought about it like that. What suddenly makes you an expert?"

"I took a photography class this spring, and a few of the girls had also done some modeling."

"Oh, so there were models in your class, huh? They wouldn't be too young for you, would they?" Stephanie said, wiggling her eyebrows.

"Nope, not too young at all." Todd grinned.

On Saturday, practice proceeded without any real problems, but all the girls were pretty quiet. Stephanie was glad when Coach Becker finally released them, and she and Alexis headed toward the parking lot where Todd waited in the van.

"Hey, did you bring your swimsuit?" Stephanie asked Alexis as they climbed in the backseat of Todd's van. Alexis looked at the lift on one side and at the wheelchair folded up against the wall. Stephanie caught Todd's eyes in the rearview mirror. She suddenly realized that she'd never told Alexis about Todd being in a wheelchair. Half the time, Stephanie herself almost forgot. Todd just seemed so normal to her . . . "or at least as abnormal as ever," she often told him.

Todd adjusted the volume as a song he liked came on the radio.

"Yes," Alexis said, "but I feel weird in a swimsuit." She paused and then said, "Hey is someone in your family disabled?"

"That would be me," Todd said as he raised his right hand off the steering wheel.

"Shut up! Really?" Alexis persisted.

"It's him," Stephanie said. "He smarted off to me once, and I let him have it good."

"These are wooden," Todd said, hitting his

kneecap while pounding the knuckles of his left hand against the window at the same time.

"He's kidding," Stephanie said. "It is his wheelchair. He was in a crash last year and is going through therapy to get him on his feet."

"You're not embarrassing me at all, Alexis," he said reassuringly. "I'd rather have people ask than ignore it. So," Todd said, changing the subject, "where shall I take you, my ladies?"

Stephanie looked at Alexis, who shrugged her shoulders.

"Just drop us off at the house, Jeeves," Stephanie said. "We'll decide what to do from there."

"As you wish," Todd replied, sounding just like Wesley from *The Princess Bride*.

When they arrived home, Todd pulled into the driveway but left the motor running.

"You're not coming in?" Alexis asked.

"No," Todd said.

"Getting together with some girls from your photography class?" Stephanie asked slyly.

"No, goofball," he replied, "I have practice with the praise band at church. I'll see you later."

"It was nice to meet you, Todd," Alexis said.

"Later," Stephanie added.

"Later," Todd said. "You two stay out of trouble."

As the girls approached the house, Alexis

whispered to Stephanie, "You should have told me about your brother. I felt so stupid when I asked about the wheelchair."

"Don't worry. Todd didn't mind."

Stephanie pulled out her key and opened the front door. As the girls walked in, Alexis gasped.

"I love your house. It's so light and open."

"Dad and Gramps had to do some serious remodeling to make room for Todd to move around in his wheelchair. But you're right. It makes the whole house feel better."

The girls stopped in the kitchen and found a note on the counter from Stephanie's mother that there was chicken salad for sandwiches in the fridge.

"I'm starved," Stephanie said. "You want something to eat?"

"Sure, whatever you're having," Alexis replied.

Stephanie made a couple of sandwiches, and they settled on stools at the island counter. Stephanie was amazed by how quickly Alexis ate. She took enormous bites of her sandwich and stuffed handfuls of chips in her mouth at a time. Stephanie was surprised that someone so thin would eat like that.

Alexis glanced up, and Stephanie quickly looked away so Alexis wouldn't know she'd been staring. After that, Alexis slowed down a bit.

"This is really good," Alexis said. "I haven't had

chicken salad in ages. My mom and I went vegetarian last year, and she's doing really well, but I don't feel like it works for me."

"I don't think I could ever go veggie," Stephanie said.

As the girls talked about school, Alexis said she was really bummed when her dad had to transfer so close to the end of the school year.

"I'm so glad you talked to me at tryouts that first day," Alexis said. "You're pretty much my only friend here."

"Just wait," Stephanie said. "Once high school starts, you'll be the most popular girl in school."

"I doubt that," Alexis said.

"Why?" Stephanie asked. "You're so pretty that half the guys will be following you around."

"I hope not," Alexis said, suddenly tense. "I mean, thanks. I guess I just don't see myself as all that pretty. I've got too much baby fat."

"Alexis," Stephanie said firmly, "you're beautiful, and you don't need to lose weight. Is that why you didn't want to go to the pool?"

"Kind of," Alexis confessed. "My mom always says I was such a cute little girl."

"Ouch."

"Yeah, I know. And modeling was fun when I was little, but lately the photographers have said I don't look 'sexy' enough. I don't want to look sexy. I mean, I'm still just a kid."

"That sounds awful," Stephanie replied, thinking about what Todd had said about models.

"Yeah, it's not really so great," Alexis agreed. "Hey, do you mind if I use your bathroom?"

"Sure. It's down the hall—first door on the right."

After finishing her sandwich, Stephanie cleaned up the kitchen. Then she flipped through her mother's copy of *Reader's Digest*. But Alexis still had not come out of the bathroom.

"Alexis," Stephanie said, finally knocking on the door, "are you OK?"

"I'll be out in a minute," Alexis called from inside.

Stephanie heard water running in the sink, and then Alexis opened the door. Stephanie was surprised by how pale her friend looked. Alexis's blotchy face was still wet.

"Are you sure you're OK?" Stephanie asked.

"Yeah," Alexis said, "sorry to be so long."

"No problem," Stephanie assured her. "I just wanted to make sure you weren't sick or something."

"No, I'm fine," she said. "Maybe we should go swimming after all."

"Great," Stephanie said, sensing Alexis wanted to change the subject.

"Will there be a lot of kids our age there?"

"No," Stephanie said, "it's my mom's best friend's pool. I think it's the only inground pool in town other than the park district one and the one at the college. My mom's friend is great. I call her Aunt Sarah."

"Oh good," Alexis said. "I don't need to worry about guys thinking I'm fat."

Stephanie stifled the urge to roll her eyes. How could Alexis be so worried about being fat? "We'll probably be alone. Aunt Sarah is usually working at her computer this time of day."

The girls put on their suits and threw on cover-ups before leaving the house to walk a block over to Aunt Sarah's. The beautiful two-story red brick house had a full porch supported by white pillars and showcasing a beautiful lilac bush at the corner. A black iron fence surrounded the property, and there was an ornate water fountain in the middle of the circular drive.

"Wow!" Alexis said. "It's like a southern mansion."

"You'll get used to it. Aunt Sarah has a flair for the dramatic. She used to teach literature at Northwestern, and now she writes romance novels."

"Must have taken quite a few books to pay for all this," Alexis observed as they walked around to the back of the house to see the beautiful pool, complete with slide and waterfall.

"Yeah, she's done pretty well for herself," Stephanie said.

At poolside, Stephanie slipped out of her sandals and cover-up. It was a hot day for May, and the pool looked really refreshing. Stephanie immediately jumped in just as a German shepherd trotted out from the bushes. He ran to the edge of the pool and barked repeatedly, running back and forth.

"Hi, Fang," Stephanie said, splashing the dog. He shook his head and almost looked like he was smiling.

"He's not mean, is he?" Alexis said, still gripping her bag and beach towel.

"No, he's a lover bear," Stephanie said. "He's the world's worst guard dog. He makes friends with everybody."

After Fang licked Alexis's hand and she was finally convinced he wasn't going to eat her alive, she dropped her cover-up on a lounge chair before jumping into the pool. Stephanie was shocked at how far the other girl's shoulder blades stuck out. Alexis was even thinner than Stephanie could have imagined.

Stephanie remembered her new friend's feeding frenzy and lengthy stay in the bathroom. Could she have been making herself throw up? As Stephanie and Alexis splashed around in the pool, Stephanie became more and more convinced that Alexis had some kind of eating disorder. She only wondered what she could do to help.

Stephanie curled up on the sofa in the open family room. She had already showered and put on her pajamas. The Saturday evening sky was now pitch-black, and it was time for the weekly ritual. Todd sat in the recliner with his legs propped up and covered in a blanket. From the kitchen both of them smelled the popcorn popping. *Creature Features* started at ten o'clock sharp. Todd and Stephanie had watched the corny old monster movies together since she was old enough not to be scared. Saturday night's menu was always the same: popcorn, orange soda, and chocolate-covered peanuts. The only thing that changed was the movie.

"What's the flick tonight?" Stephanie asked.

"*The Incredible Shrinking Man*," Todd replied. "We've seen it before."

"Good, so you won't mind if I talk during the movie?" she asked.

"Not like it matters what I think, motor-mouth," he said.

Stephanie threw a handful of popcorn at him.

"Not on the new sofa!" her mother called from the doorway. "I'm headed up to bed. Don't stay up too late."

"We won't," Todd and Stephanie chimed.

Stephanie sat quietly through the opening sequence and then said, trying to sound casual, "So Alexis and I went swimming today."

"So?" Todd replied, munching on popcorn.

"Well, I think there's something wrong with her."

"What do you mean, wrong?" Todd asked.

"She ate lunch here, and then I think she went into the bathroom and made herself puke," Stephanie explained. "Then at Aunt Sarah's, when she took off her cover-up, I could practically see her skeleton."

"Sounds anorexic," said Todd. "So what are you going to do?"

Stephanie rested her head on her brother's shoulder. "I don't know. For starters, I'm going to pray. I don't want to tackle something like this without asking for God's help first."

"Sounds like a plan," Todd said. "I'll pray too—after the movie. I actually think this one is a remake that we haven't seen."

CHAPTER:05

"I can't believe it's the first game of the season already," Alexis told Stephanie the following Saturday morning. It was in the high eighties, and the grass around the ball field was bone dry.

The Lincoln Sluggers were one of the best teams around. They'd gone to regionals for eight years in a row and state three times. The way practices had been going, Stephanie didn't think the Chapel Hill Saints had a chance. Jackie's dad had made the promised appearance at their last practice and shouted at Coach Becker in the parking lot. The girls couldn't hear the entire argument, but could easily pick out words like "my money," "investment," and "ludicrous." Coach Becker never raised his voice.

Stephanie was glad her parents had made the trip to watch the game, but hated for them to see the mess the team was in. Alexis's parents were there too. Stephanie had met them at a practice earlier in the week. They seemed nice enough, but Stephanie was surprised to hear Alexis's mom complain that the softball uniform made Alexis look fat. That was the last thing her friend needed to hear.

Stephanie noticed that her parents were sitting with Mr. and Mrs. Wilson. She also saw, much to her dismay, that Jackie's mom and dad sat directly behind her parents.

"Maybe they'll all get to be best friends," Alexis said sarcastically when she saw where Stephanie was looking.

"Somehow I don't think Mr. Wolfe will be real thrilled to hear about Dad's Mr. Potato Head collection," Stephanie replied. "Let's go. Jennifer is waving us over."

Stephanie resisted the urge to laugh when she saw Heather and Jackie sitting on the bench.

You got what you wanted, Heather, she thought. *You and Jackie get to spend lots of quality time together.*

The Saints were up to bat first. Natalie, Amanda, and Jenny quickly struck out.

After a discouraging top of the first, the Saints made their way to the field. As Alexis prepared to throw her first pitch, Stephanie whispered a prayer out in left field. She clapped her hands, trying to rouse her team, but everyone else looked discouraged or irritated.

Alexis wound up for the pitch, amazing Stephanie with the power behind her throw. She watched as the batter hit the ball. It flew into center field, over Amanda's head, and far into the outfield. Amanda darted into the field to retrieve the ball as the Sluggers batter ran to first base and headed for second base. Amanda threw the ball to second base, but there wasn't enough force behind it. Mollie had to run for the ball, and by the time she retrieved it, the runner was safely on second.

"Nice hustle," Stephanie called, but even she could hear the insincerity in her voice. Unless Alexis's pitching could save them, they were in big trouble.

Alexis faced the next batter. She pitched, and the batter hit the ball into right field. Foul ball. But the girl on second had already started her run for third. She raced back toward second, but Stephanie could see she intended to steal third. Alexis must have spotted the move too, because as she made the motion to pitch, she turned and threw the ball to second. Mollie, however, was watching the batter and missed the ball. The Sluggers girl saw the opportunity to steal third, and ran. Mollie quickly gathered the ball and threw it to third, forcing the girl back to second, but only barely.

"Watch what you're doing," Amanda yelled at Mollie from center field.

"I will when you watch where you're throwing," Mollie retorted.

"Mollie," Stephanie said, "ignore her."

"Mind your own business," Amanda said.

"You're right, Steph," Mollie said, and they both turned away from Amanda.

Alexis prepared to pitch again. Coach Becker called out encouragement, but Amanda was now bickering with Jenny on first base. As the next batter entered the box, Alexis wound up for the pitch. She threw a beautiful strike ball right into the catcher's glove while the batter took a full swing at air.

"Strike one," the umpire called as Natalie threw the ball back to Alexis.

"Excellent, Alexis," the coach called out to her, clapping. Stephanie was sure her friend had to be encouraged.

Alexis wound up for another pitch. Releasing with an underhand snap, the ball again sailed past the batter, who took a full swing. But Natalie missed the ball, and it rolled behind her. The Sluggers runner on second took advantage of the catcher's fumble and darted toward third base. The entire team watched as Natalie grabbed for the ball and followed Alexis's calls to throw to third. But by the time she did, the runner had tagged the base safely.

Stephanie wanted to tell Natalie it was OK. After

all, this was her first game to play catcher. But she heard Heather call from the dugout, "I thought we learned how to catch a ball in kindergarten, Natalie."

Natalie crouched back into position, shaking her head. Stephanie turned her attention back to Alexis, who was showing signs of early fatigue. Her next pitch was beautiful—for the batter. The girl at bat struck the ball in mid-swing, sending it far into the outfield, beyond the fence that designated the park boundaries. The batter threw her bat to the ground and ran for first, but when she saw that she had hit a home run, she slowed down to a jog. The runner on third, however, ran at full speed to cross home plate. The game was now 2–0. The Sluggers fans cheered wildly.

Alexis's shoulders drooped. She stood still as the next batter stepped up to the plate. Stephanie swayed nervously in left field, hoping and praying that Alexis could keep it together and get this inning over with. Alexis took her time and focused on her pitch. She stepped back gracefully, balancing her body. Raising her arm in front of her, she rocked back and forth before spinning her arm behind her in one complete windmill turn. She released the ball, and it flew at the batter.

"Strike one!" the umpire called out.

"Strike two!" she again called out a moment later.

Alexis again took her time, and when she pitched the next ball and it made contact with the catcher's glove, the team all sighed in relief as they heard the umpire call, "Strike three! You're out!"

Next up to the plate was a girl who looked eighteen. She was over six feet tall and solid muscle. Stephanie worried about how far this girl could hit a ball if she made contact. Fortunately, Alexis made sure she didn't and struck her out. The inning was over. Stephanie and her team headed for their benches.

"Great job, Alexis," Coach Becker said, patting her on the shoulder.

Stephanie was relieved to see her exhausted friend smile. Stephanie walked to the cooler and reached down to open it. As she did, Jackie sat down on the lid while a couple of her friends giggled. When Stephanie looked up, she and Jackie locked eyes.

"Is something wrong?" Jackie asked sweetly.

"No, nothing's wrong at all, except that there seems to be a snake sitting on the cooler," Stephanie replied. Amanda giggled, and Jackie shot her an icy glare. Amanda stopped mid-giggle, but Stephanie sensed she was now the one in power.

Jackie's face turned white. Everyone in the bull pen was now staring at them. Stephanie's temples pulsed in anger. She was so sick of Jackie, but she forced her face to remain calm.

After a long moment, Jackie stood up. She looked at Stephanie and said, "Sticks and stones may break my bones, but at least I'm not a cripple like your loser brother." Then she walked away with all the dignity she could manage.

Stephanie gritted her teeth and opened the cooler to get a drink for herself and Alexis. She looked up and saw everyone staring. Heather sneered when their eyes met, but Amanda looked surprised and shocked.

You may have gone a little too far with that last comment, Jackie, thought Stephanie, *even for your little worker bees.*

As Stephanie walked down the dugout, she glanced up in the stands to see her parents on the first row of bleachers and Todd sitting next to them in his wheelchair. She knew better than to let Jackie's words hurt her, but her heart did ache for Todd. He didn't complain too often, but she knew it was hard for him to deal with all of it—the pain, not being able to walk, losing the chance to play college ball, even wondering if he'd ever have another girlfriend. She couldn't believe Jackie was so desperate to impress people that she'd stoop so low. But as she looked up, Todd winked at her, and she smiled. She was grateful for the relationship they had—a relationship that would have been much different if he hadn't had the accident.

"Hey," Stephanie said to Alexis, handing her a sports drink, "drink some of this."

"Thanks," Alexis replied with a soft smile. "You know, I'm not really into boxing, but I think you just threw a knockout punch." She nodded toward Jackie, who sat alone.

Stephanie shrugged. She watched as Alexis carefully read the nutritional data on the label before opening the cap and taking a drink.

"You feel OK?" Stephanie asked.

"Yeah," Alexis said, "I'm just a little tired."

Stephanie sat down next to her, knowing neither would be up to bat for a while. She really felt like she had to let Alexis know she was worried about her.

"So, can I ask you something?" Stephanie said.

"Sure," Alexis said, "what's up?"

"Well," Stephanie hesitated, "it's just that—don't get me wrong, I think you're beautiful and a terrific pitcher—but I'm a little worried about your weight."

"I know, I know," Alexis said, "I really need to lose a few pounds. You don't need to remind me."

"Alexis," Stephanie pleaded, "that's not what I mean! I mean, I think you're too thin, not too fat!"

"What are you saying?" Alexis asked angrily. "That I have anorexia or something?"

That's exactly what I'm saying, thought Stephanie, but she could tell Alexis wasn't ready to hear that. "No one said anything about an eating disorder. I just wanted to tell you that—"

"What are you, my mother? a doctor?" Alexis demanded. "No, I don't think so. So I think you can just leave me alone."

"But—"

"Drop it," Alexis insisted.

Stephanie noticed that some of the other girls were now watching them and decided that she should just drop it, at least for the time being. She knew Alexis wanted to be left alone, but there wasn't really anywhere for her to go.

Stephanie was relieved to hear Coach Becker say, "Swift, on deck."

Stephanie walked over, put on her helmet, and readied herself to enter the batter's box. Mollie swung and struck out. She turned away from the field and walked back to the fence, passing Stephanie.

"Good luck," Mollie said.

"Thanks, Mollie," Stephanie said, "and don't let it get to you. This just isn't our day!"

"I'll say," Mollie muttered.

Stephanie entered the batter's box and gripped her bat, winding it up and stretching out. She took a couple of practice swings before stepping to the plate. She watched the pitcher. It was the tall girl she thought would hit a ball into orbit. She made eye contact and watched the other girl carefully.

"Strike one," the umpire called.

Where did that come from? Stephanie thought. *Focus. Eyes on the ball.*

Stephanie realized she wasn't paying attention. Alexis was the main thing on her mind. Stephanie hadn't meant to hurt her, but that's exactly what she'd done.

"Strike two."

"Loser," she heard someone in her own dugout call out. She couldn't tell whether it was Jackie or Heather.

Wake up, girl! You can't do this to your team.

The pitcher wound up and prepared to release the ball. Stephanie tried to concentrate. She watched carefully as the ball left the pitcher's mound and sped toward her. She swung. The bat made contact with the ball and sent it far into left field. She dropped her bat and raced to first base as the Sluggers left fielder threw the ball to the shortstop, who threw it to first base. But Stephanie was safe! Her team and the bleachers cheered.

As it turned out, that was the highlight of her day. The next batter, Elise, struck out and brought the team to the outfield still trailing. It was strange, but during the times when the Saints rode the bench, Alexis retreated from Stephanie. At one point, Alexis actually sat next to Jackie, having what appeared to be a friendly conversation, which made sense in no universe Stephanie could imagine. By the top of the seventh inning, the score was 9–0 Sluggers. The game was over.

While most of the parents waited in the parking lot, Coach Becker took a few moments to talk to the team about the game.

"I'm disappointed," Coach Becker said. "You ladies didn't play like a team. There was no heart or joy in this game, and that's why we lost."

Stephanie knew Coach Becker was right. It was the most miserable experience Stephanie had ever had—even worse than the time when she was five and ended up with a bloody nose during a soccer game.

On the ride home, Stephanie and Todd sat quietly in the backseat. Stephanie reached into her gym bag to grab her sports drink and pulled out a piece of paper. Unfolding it, she was surprised to read its message:

"Why don't you just quit and spare everyone your goody-goody attitude. All you do in the outfield is graze, you fat cow."

Terrific, thought Stephanie. *Now I'm getting hate mail!*

"What's wrong?" Todd whispered.

Stephanie glanced up at her parents in the front seat. She really wasn't in the mood to explain everything to them. She slipped her brother the note. As he read it, his eyes widened in surprise and then narrowed in anger. He started to say something, but Stephanie stopped him.

"Later," she mouthed.

Todd nodded and gave her hand a squeeze.

CHAPTER:06

On Monday morning Stephanie looked at herself in the mirror a long time. If Alexis thought Alexis was fat, what did she think about Stephanie? Was she missing something? Did other people really think she was fat? She'd read over the note about twenty times that weekend, wondering why someone would call her a fat cow. She knew it was probably just a way to hurt her, but still, she worried.

At last she got dressed and went down to the kitchen. She started to grab one of the donuts on the counter and then stopped. She reached for a banana instead. Her mom sat at the breakfast table, drinking a cup of tea and reading the paper.

"Hey, Mom," Stephanie said, "can I ask you a question—and promise me you'll be honest?"

"Of course, sweetheart," her mom said, lowering the paper. "What is it?"

"Do you think I'm fat?" Stephanie asked, turning

around slowly to let her mom get a good look.

"You? Fat?" her mom questioned. "Honey, there isn't an ounce of fat on your body."

Stephanie looked doubtful. "Are you just saying that?" she asked her mom.

"No, I'm not just saying that!" her mom reassured her. "What's this about?"

"Alexis, that girl on my softball team, is always talking about how fat she is. I must weigh at least twenty pounds more than she does. I don't want to look like . . . like some fat cow."

"I don't want you *ever* to use those kinds of words to describe yourself, Stephanie," her mom said. She stood and put her arms around her daughter. "You're beautiful, and you have the body shape that God designed just for you. Throughout your whole life you'll meet women who worry too much about their weight. You can't let their negative self-images affect how you think about yourself."

"My whole life? Really?"

"Absolutely. I even heard your grandmother the other day complaining about her thighs. For many women, it never ends."

The thought of her grandmother worrying about her thighs made Alexis smile. How silly!

"Thanks, Mom," Stephanie said. She hugged her mother and headed for the door.

"Hey, young lady," her mom said, "you need some breakfast. At least take a piece of toast."

Stephanie ate the toast with peanut butter and jelly as she walked to school. She hoped her last week of school would be better than last weekend. At least Matt would be there to make her laugh. She hadn't seen him since Friday because he'd been on a youth group retreat for kids about to go to high school. She had to miss it because of the game.

Stephanie wished she'd never gone out for softball. The Chapel Hill Saints certainly weren't living up to their name. Now that even Alexis had stopped talking to her, she'd give anything to skip Wednesday's practice. Mr. Meyers in American history had given her the perfect excuse.

"Ladies and gentlemen," Mr. Meyers said, "just a reminder that on Thursday, we will take the last test of the year. It will be a cumulative exam of everything we have studied over the past semester, including dates of all significant events, with both short answer and essay questions. I suggest you take this exam very seriously; it's a significant portion of your final grade."

Mr. Meyers was a good teacher, but Stephanie thought he took an unnatural delight in watching his students squirm. Stephanie glanced down at her school calendar. She had forgotten to write down the date of the test.

"I should have started studying weeks ago!" she complained to Matt at lunch. They sat at a table by themselves. Usually they hung out with a bunch of Matt's friends, who had kind of adopted Stephanie as a kid sister. But most of them were on a field trip that day, so it was just the two of them.

"What's the big deal?" Matt asked. "You've done great all semester. This will be review for you."

"It's the dates. I hate dates! Will you help me study, Matty?" Stephanie asked.

"Sure," he said. "But I never knew you hated dates so much."

"Hate, despise, loathe, detest," she said, taking a bite of her sandwich. "So, how was your weekend?"

"The retreat was great," he said. "Wish you could have been there."

Matt looked at her with an expression that she couldn't quite read, but it made her uncomfortable. She looked away.

"Believe me, I wish I could have been there too. The game was a disaster." She told him what had happened, both on and off the field.

"I just kept wishing you were there to make me laugh and forget about all of it," she said. When she looked up, Matt wore the same expression—intense, almost questioning.

"Do you mean that?" he said.

"Of course," she replied, feeling a little confused. She decided to change the subject. Things were getting a little weird between them, and she couldn't handle that on top of everything else. "Want to study tonight? Around seven o'clock?"

"Why don't I just walk you home from school and we'll study then?"

"Um, sure," Stephanie said. "Todd should be there, so that will be fine."

"Since when do we need a chaperone?" Matt joked.

"That's the rule," she said. "No boys in the house without adult supervision—if you can really call Todd an adult."

"What does your mom think we'll do? Make out or something?" Matt asked.

Stephanie turned bright red. "No, no, nothing like that. It's just . . . just that—"

"It's OK, Steph," Matt said, laughing, "I was kidding. My mom has the same rule too."

But he was looking at her again in that weird way.

"See you after school," Stephanie said and practically ran out of the cafeteria, leaving Matt with a confused look on his face.

It was a good thing Stephanie's afternoon classes were mainly wrap-up and review, because between worrying about the history exam, the problem with Alexis, and what was going on with Matt, Stephanie found it hard to focus. Plus, it had finally dawned on her that this was the last week of middle school—the last time she'd walk down these halls, the last time she'd have crazy Mr. Ross for biology, the last time she'd see some of her friends. Nothing would ever be the same again.

Matt waited at her locker after school, and they walked toward her house together. It had cooled off, and in every front yard flowers bloomed and filled the air with their fragrance.

"Are you ready to review the history of our great nation from the Civil War to the present?" Matt asked, mimicking Mr. Meyers's deep voice.

"Yes, sir," Stephanie replied. "Everything except Vietnam and the Watergate mess."

"Indeed, Miss Swift," Matt said, still impersonating Mr. Meyers. "Those were not shining moments in our country's history. But those who do not study history are doomed to repeat it."

Stephanie laughed. "He always says that! What does it mean anyway? It seems to me like people make the same mistakes over and over, whether they study the past or not. Look at all the wars we have to memorize the dates for. I hate dates."

"Yes, you've made that very clear," Matt replied.

"Anyway, let's wait to start the review until after we've had something to eat. My brain needs fortification."

Stephanie was surprised to see her mom, not Todd, at home when they arrived.

"I keep forgetting you're already off work for the summer," she said, kissing her mom in the front hall. "Is it OK if Matt and I study for a while? We've got a big history test on Thursday."

"Of course!" she said, hugging Matt too. "Although it takes more self-discipline than I have to study on a beautiful spring afternoon like this."

"We'll sit on the porch," Stephanie said, "and catch the breeze."

"Or shoot it," Matt said. Stephanie grinned. She loved Matt's sense of humor.

They spent most of the afternoon looking over their notes on President Lincoln, General Lee, and General Sherman.

"Remember how Mr. Meyers said that Sherman's march through Georgia was the beginning of modern warfare?" Stephanie asked.

"Sounds like an essay question to me," Matt replied, jotting it down.

They sped through their notes on the second half of the nineteenth century and had just gotten to World War I when Stephanie's mom announced that dinner was ready.

"Want to stay for supper, Matt?" she asked. "We're having chicken enchiladas."

"Sounds fantastic, Mrs. Swift, but I'd better get home. Mom asked me to mow the lawn tonight."

Stephanie felt strangely disappointed that Matt was leaving. "See you tomorrow," she said, and went to give him his usual good-bye hug. But instead of hugging her back, Matt just patted her awkwardly on the shoulder.

"Bye, Steph," he said, and headed out the door.

After dinner, Stephanie studied some more, plus worked on a few remaining assignments for other classes. She was trying to figure out whether she should go to softball practice Wednesday night or not. The truth was that she really didn't want to, but she didn't want to just use the history test as an excuse. After all, Coach Becker had been pretty clear about the time commitment to the team. She just hadn't known what kind of team she was committing to.

Stephanie put off the decision until Wednesday afternoon. She and Matt were sitting on the porch again, trying to focus on history. But mostly, they just talked about the end of school and what high school might be like.

Stephanie's mom stuck her head out and said, "I'm planning an early dinner so you can get to practice, Steph. What time do you need to leave?"

Stephanie looked down at her notes. For all of their studying, they'd only made it through World War II. "I don't know, Mom," she said. "We've got this test tomorrow, and I really need to study some more. Do you think it would be OK if I missed practice tonight?"

Stephanie could practically see the wheels spinning in her mother's head. Her mom had two separate but equally sure convictions: her children should keep their commitments and they should do well in school. Which would win out in this case?

"I don't like for you to miss practice," her mom said. "But, OK—just this once. Be sure to call Coach Becker and tell him you won't be there though."

Ugh. She hadn't counted on that. The last thing she wanted to do was call Coach Becker.

"OK," she reluctantly agreed. "Thanks."

A few minutes later, Todd wheeled in. "Missed you at the pool today, sis," he said.

"Sorry, Todd," she began, "Matt and I've been studying for this test and—"

"It's OK," he said. "It's good to see you haven't been lonely." He grinned at Matt.

"My sister says your therapy's been going really well," Matt said.

"Yeah, she's been so encouraging."

Stephanie looked back and forth between them.

Todd? And Matt's sister Becky? Stephanie raised her eyebrows at Todd, who just grinned and shrugged his shoulders.

"Hey," Todd said, "can I help it if chicks dig my minivan?" He rolled back into the kitchen, leaving Matt and Stephanie giggling.

"Hey," Matt said, "as long as you're ditching softball practice, you should ditch the game on Saturday too, and come to the youth group cookout. It's the first high school thing we're invited to. We're going Frisbee golfing afterward."

"I don't know, Matt. Mom wasn't too jazzed about me missing practice. I think missing the game isn't an option." As it turned out, it was her only option.

"Swift," Coach said on the phone, "I have a policy: no practice, no game. If you're not coming tonight, don't bother to show up on Saturday."

Even though she hated to hear the irritation in her coach's voice, Stephanie was relieved she could attend the cookout instead of the game.

"Maybe you should just quit if you're so miserable," Matt told her after she got off the phone.

"I don't know. I hate to just give up like that," she said. "Although I think I'd be happy never to see any of those people again."

Then she thought about Alexis. Alexis needed a

friend, even if she didn't know it. Stephanie knew she couldn't quit the team.

Thanks to all their studying, Stephanie was pretty sure she aced the history exam the next day.

"Even the dates?" Matt asked.

"Yeah," she said. "I guess dates aren't so bad after all."

"I'm glad to hear you say that," Matt said mysteriously.

Stephanie's last day of school passed without much fanfare. Graduation would be next Tuesday, so that would be the real good-bye.

On Saturday the youth group cookout didn't go as well. The food was great, and everyone was really friendly, but she felt a little out of it. The rest of the graduating eighth graders had been on the retreat together, and they kept laughing about how much fun they'd had. Stephanie was especially irritated by a girl named Cassandra who managed to sit between her and Matt at lunch. Stephanie just picked at her hamburger.

"And then," Cassandra said to Stephanie, laughing so hard she could barely talk, "Matt said, 'When you catch the breeze, don't shoot it!' Isn't that funny?"

"Yeah," said Stephanie, staring intently at a potato chip, "hysterical."

Why was she so mad? What did she care if Matt told the same stupid joke to Cassandra? Without finishing her food, Stephanie abruptly left the table and threw her plate into the trash. She should have known this was a bad idea. She'd ditched her game, and as her mother always told her, "Nothing good happens when you shirk your responsibilities."

Matt ran over to her. "You coming with us to play Frisbee golf?"

"By 'us' do you mean Cassandra?" she asked.

Matt looked startled. "Yeah, I mean, I guess she's going."

"I don't think so, Matt. I'll just head home. My dad will be by in a few minutes."

"Oh," he said, "OK then. See you tomorrow."

Stephanie watched as he returned to his place next to Cassandra. Then she pulled out her cell phone to call her dad.

"Can you come and pick me up now?" she asked.

"I thought you were staying another hour or two," he said. "No Frisbee golf?"

"I'm not in the mood," she said.

"All right, but I'm in the middle of varnishing my new display case. It will be a few minutes before I can finish the section I'm on and clean up. I'll get there as soon as I can."

So Stephanie had to watch as the rest of the kids piled into church vans and headed for the Frisbee golf course. Matt waved to her as he got in, but no one else really said much. She wandered inside the church to wait for her dad. The building was quiet and had that creepy, empty feeling big buildings have when no one is bustling around. Stephanie heard footsteps and turned around to see her pastor's wife.

"What are you doing here, Stephanie?" Carrie asked.

"The cookout just ended, and everyone else headed out to play Frisbee golf. I'm waiting for my dad to pick me up."

"Is he on his way?" Carrie asked.

"No, he had to finish up a project first."

"Why don't you call him back and tell him I'll give you a ride home?"

Stephanie grinned. "That would be great," she said, and pulled out her cell phone.

Stephanie had ridden in Carrie's car only once before, when her parents had asked Carrie to give Stephanie a ride home from the hospital one night. But when they walked out to the parking lot, Stephanie didn't see it anywhere.

"Where's the Miata?" she asked.

"Sold it," Carrie said. "We traded it in for a minivan."

Stephanie smiled. "Todd says minivans are great for picking up girls."

"That sounds like your brother," Carrie said wryly, pulling out her keys. "They certainly are useful for carrying extra people around."

Stephanie couldn't understand why Carrie was grinning. "Can you keep a secret?" Carrie asked.

"Definitely," Stephanie replied.

"Jeff and I are having a baby!"

"That's awesome!" Stephanie said. "You guys will make terrific parents. Can I babysit?"

"Absolutely," Carrie said.

As they drove to Stephanie's house, Carrie asked her if she'd had a good time at youth group that afternoon.

"It was OK," Stephanie said, unable to hide her lack of enthusiasm.

"What's wrong?"

Stephanie thought for a moment. "Can you keep a secret?" Stephanie asked.

"Seems only fair," Carrie replied.

Stephanie took a deep breath and told Carrie everything—all the stuff going on with Alexis and Jackie, her fears about high school, her concerns about Todd, and even . . .

"I think I'm starting to like Matt Ford as more than just a friend," she said.

"Wow!" said Carrie. "That wasn't just one secret. I think that was about twenty."

"So what should I do?" Stephanie asked.

"About which thing?"

"About everything!" Stephanie said.

Carrie thought for a moment. "As far as the softball team thing goes, I think you need to stick it out. Stay friends with Alexis, but don't push her too hard about the eating disorder. You might want to mention it to your coach though. Sounds like you've handled the Jackie aspect of it really well. Unfortunately, there are lots of people like that out there. The funny thing is, though, that sometimes the people who act the cruelest are the ones who are the most insecure. You may find a way of getting through to Jackie too."

"What about Matt?" Stephanie still couldn't believe she'd actually told anyone about her feelings for him.

"I'm not sure. We might just have to wait and see about that one. And don't let what happened tonight give you a bad feeling about the youth group. It can be hard to get to know a new group of kids, but I think you'll really like them once you do."

"It's just that I seem to have a hard time making friends. I know tons of people, but I'm not close to many of them, especially not the girls. Todd and Matt are my best friends."

"Hmm," said Carrie, "I see what you mean. You want to hear my theory?"

"Love to," Stephanie replied.

"Some people look like they have tons of friends, but it's not really true. Some people hang on to their friends by going along with everything their friends say, and some people keep friends by intimidating the people around them."

Stephanie thought of Jackie and Alexis. "I think I know what you mean."

"My guess is," Carrie said, "that you're not willing to use either of those methods. So until the people around you grow up a little, you may not have many close friendships."

"That's not really encouraging," Stephanie said.

"I know," Carrie replied. "I didn't have a group of really close friends until my high school youth group. Even then some kids were really immature, but I was able to make some great relationships with other people my age who really loved God and were trying to do the right thing. And remember that even enemies can sometimes become friends."

By that time they had pulled into Stephanie's driveway. "Thanks, Carrie," Stephanie said, "for everything. And congratulations!"

On Monday night after Stephanie ate dinner, she dressed in her practice clothes and gathered her gear. Alone in her room, she hesitated and then knelt beside her bed.

Hi, God, she prayed silently, *I'm really nervous about tonight, and I don't really even want to go. I don't want to deal with Jackie, and I know Alexis won't want to deal with me. Please be with me and help me get through it. And, Lord, if you think it's cool for me to like Matt more than a friend, could you let me know? Thanks for helping Todd to get better and walk again someday. Amen.*

When Stephanie's dad dropped her off at practice, she was surprised to see Alexis sitting next to Jackie. She didn't know how Jackie had managed to get her hooks into Alexis, but she knew it was *not* a good thing. Stephanie sat down alone.

She was surprised when Mollie sat down next to her. Soon Elise and Natalie had joined her, and they told her all about Saturday's game. Evidently, it hadn't been much different than their last game, except that Alexis didn't pitch as well and Jackie got more time on the mound.

"The way Jackie told it," Mollie said, "she was doing Alexis some big favor."

"It's like Jackie and Alexis are best friends all of a sudden," Elise said.

"Yeah, and I know someone who isn't happy about it," Natalie said, nodding her head toward Amanda, who was sitting alone and scowling at Jackie and Alexis.

Stephanie hated herself for listening to this gossip, but she was also glad to get an idea of what had been going on.

"Anyway," Mollie said, "we're glad you're back, Steph."

Stephanie smiled. Maybe this wasn't going to be so bad after all. But when she looked over at Alexis, she felt anxious. Alexis looked really bad. Her cheeks were sunken in, and she looked so pale.

Coach Becker called for their attention. "So here's the deal, ladies. I've never before coached a team with so much talent and so little enthusiasm. I'm not enjoying coaching you, and it's obvious that most of you are not enjoying playing. It's time to put personal differences aside. It's time to tell your parents to stop calling me to get you better positions on the team." He looked right at Jackie when he made that comment, and most of the girls did the same. "Starting tonight, I want to see a new attitude. We'll either start playing as a team, or we'll stop playing altogether. It's up to you."

Jackie whispered something to Alexis. Stephanie watched them, and so did Coach Becker.

"When I'm talking, ladies," Coach Becker said, "pay attention." Alexis's face went from white to red, but Jackie looked smug. "Now let's have a better practice, and let's think about the team instead of ourselves. Take your field positions."

The girls rose and made their way to their practice teams. Stephanie stopped, pretending to tie her shoe, and waited until Alexis passed by. She gently touched her on the arm.

"Hey, Alexis," Stephanie said, "I'm sorry if I made you mad the other day. I just wanted to make sure you're doing OK. I'm worried about you."

"Are you?" Alexis asked. "I wouldn't think so by the mail I've been getting."

"I have no idea what you're talking about," Stephanie replied.

"I think I can figure out for myself who my real friends are," Alexis said, and walked over to where Jackie waited for her.

Stephanie grabbed her glove and made her way into the outfield, feeling hurt and confused. As she passed by Alexis and Jackie, Jackie smiled that awful, fake smile at her. Stephanie, who had never hit anyone in her life, had an almost irresistible urge to punch her. But she controlled herself and ground her hand into her glove instead.

The rest of practice actually went pretty well.

Evidently, even Jackie had listened to Coach Becker's speech, and everyone got along just fine that night—or seemed to. Mollie, Elise, and Natalie continued to be friendly to Stephanie. But Stephanie could hardly stand to see how attached Alexis had gotten to Jackie.

When Stephanie got home, she went out on the back porch and plopped down next to Todd.

"So . . . practice went well, huh?" Todd asked.

"Yeah," she said, "terrific, if you're into misery."

"That bad?"

Stephanie told him all about it. "The thing is, Todd, I just don't know what to do. I mean, do I just back off and let Alexis get hurt by Jackie? Do I talk to Coach Becker? Do I take karate lessons and then go teach Jackie Wolfe a lesson?"

"Option three, definitely," Todd said. "You'd look cool in one of those white outfits."

"Seriously, I need your help."

"Good to know that at last you can acknowledge the wisdom of your far superior older brother."

"At least you got the old part right," she said. "Now, what do I do?"

"I have ancient wisdom to offer you, my child," he said, and rolled over to a bookcase on which he kept several devotional books. Stephanie knew the porch was his favorite place for quiet time.

"Here's a really great prayer I discovered in my reading last week. It's by Francis of Assisi. Read this."

Todd handed her the book and pointed to the words on the right-hand page: "Lord, make me an instrument of your peace; where there is hatred, let me sow love; where there is injury, pardon; where there is doubt, faith; where there is despair, hope; where there is darkness, light; where there is sadness, joy. Grant that I may not so much seek to be consoled as to console; to be understood as to understand; to be loved as to love. For it is in giving that we receive, it is in pardoning that we are pardoned, and it is in dying that we are born to eternal life. Amen."

Stephanie studied it carefully for several long moments. "I'm not really into the whole dying thing, but the rest of it was great," Stephanie said. "It's just so hard. Jackie's just like some kind of . . . I don't know, poison, on the team. How do I fight against that?"

"Sounds like you already have," Todd said.

"How do you mean?"

"At first, everyone was really awful, right? And now, at least those three girls you mentioned—Mollie and the other two—see you for who you are and see Jackie for who she is."

"What about Alexis?" Stephanie asked.

"I think the best thing we can do for Alexis is to pray," Todd said.

The two of them prayed together about the situation for several minutes.

"Thanks," she said. "That makes me feel better." She stood up. "'Night, Toddy."

"'Night, Steph."

CHAPTER:07

Stephanie had almost convinced herself that she should quit the softball team. Why put up with everything? But the next day she copied Francis of Assisi's prayer onto a note card and read it over and over before putting it into her pocket. Maybe God had put her on that team to bring some peace, to spread love, to help Alexis get better. She even read the prayer a few times that night during graduation, while sitting through a particularly long and boring speech by the assistant principal. She put the prayer into her practice uniform pocket that night. She figured she could use the reminder at Wednesday's practice.

When she arrived, the coach was already on the field, talking to the practice assistants and marking off an area between second and third base for shortstop practice. Stephanie walked toward the bleachers and witnessed Jackie pulling her hand out of Coach Becker's bag. Jackie looked up at Stephanie in shock and then hurried away.

What is she up to? Stephanie wondered, but she didn't want to risk getting caught going through Coach Becker's bag just to find out.

Jackie sat down near Alexis, but Heather and Amanda sat on either side of Jackie. Alexis appeared uncomfortable and refused to look at Stephanie as she passed. Stephanie decided it wasn't a good idea to talk to Alexis with Jackie right there, so she sat down next to Mollie and Elise. Natalie soon joined them, lugging a bag of equipment.

"I wish this catcher's gear wasn't so heavy," she complained.

Coach Becker entered the dugout, whistling. He seemed to be in a much better mood. Stephanie didn't blame him for being grouchy before. She wouldn't want to coach this team either.

"We're beginning our practice a little differently today, girls," he said. "Outfielders, you'll work on throwing and catching. Head on out with Jennifer."

The game of catch was actually pretty fun. Stephanie noticed that by far she had the best distance and accuracy.

"Wow," said Elise, who was her partner, "you're awesome."

"Thanks," Stephanie said, smiling.

After a half hour, Coach Becker blew his whistle. "Time to run some laps, ladies," he said. They all groaned, but there was no arguing.

Stephanie, who was in great shape from helping Todd with all his therapy, had no problem keeping up with the pace. But she noticed that Alexis was really struggling. Jackie, who had started out next to Alexis, was also near the front of the pack, and just laughed when Alexis asked her to wait up.

Stephanie slowed her pace as much as she could, hoping Alexis would catch up with her. Finally she did, but she wouldn't even look over at Stephanie. After a few moments, Alexis said, "Stop pretending like you're my friend. I don't need your pity."

Stephanie stopped dead in her tracks.

"What's wrong, Miss Swift?" Coach asked. "I think I made it clear that you were to be running laps."

Stephanie took a deep breath and hoped her voice didn't shake when she replied.

"Sorry, Coach," she said and resumed jogging.

By that time she was half the circumference of the field behind most of the runners, and Jackie and Amanda actually lapped her, laughing as they ran by. Stephanie felt like crying and just wanted to leave the track, but she knew she couldn't. She just didn't understand what she'd done to make Alexis so angry.

Coach Becker blew his whistle a few minutes

later, but to the team's dismay, they weren't finished running. The girls were lined up at the batter's box. Jennifer gave a quick blast of her whistle, signaling the first girl in line to advance to first base. This went on until each girl on the team had run the bases all the way around.

"What *is* this?" Elise asked Stephanie, panting as they both reached the back of the line. "Is Coach planning to kill us so he can enjoy the rest of his summer?"

"He did seem unusually cheerful when we got here," Stephanie replied.

Next they divided into their usual practice teams. Before Stephanie even had time to catch her breath, she heard Jennifer say, "Swift, you're up."

Stephanie noticed that Alexis was in the dugout, even though she usually pitched for the other team. She looked absolutely sick. As Stephanie grabbed her batter's helmet, she saw that Jackie had taken Alexis's place on the pitcher's mound.

As Stephanie entered the batter's box, Jackie glared at her. The first pitch came so close to Stephanie that she had to jump back to miss it.

"Ball one!" Jennifer called.

The next pitch was a strike, and Stephanie hated the smirk on Jackie's face. Jackie wound up the ball, pitched, and Stephanie swung. She felt her bat make contact and watched the ball sailing across the field and over the fence. She'd just hit her first home run! She glanced at Jackie, whose smirk was gone, and then rounded the bases. Her bench cheered, and even Natalie, who was in the outfield, hollered, "Good one, Steph!"

Stephanie felt great as they entered the dugout for their post-practice talk from Coach Becker.

"Ladies," Coach Becker said as soon as they were seated, "we have a problem." He held up a folded piece of paper and waved it at the girls. "It seems some of you aren't happy with me. Now I had hoped that we would all be able to get over the past and move forward. I thought today was a really good practice and that you all worked hard. But someone has violated my privacy. One of you left a little note for me today, and I'm not real happy about it."

Stephanie immediately looked over at Jackie, who looked back at her with an expression of fear mixed with defiance.

So that's what you were doing in his gym bag, Stephanie thought.

"Here, let me share it with you all," the coach said. "'Becker, you are a terrible coach, and none of the girls like you. Why don't you quit now so that we can have a decent season? Maybe if we had a better coach, we would win some games. LEAVE!'"

The girls gasped and mumbled to each other in disbelief. Stephanie was still staring at Jackie when she saw Alexis, sitting next to Jackie, raise her hand.

"Do you have something to say, Alexis?" Coach Becker asked.

"Coach," Alexis said, "I got a note too the other day. Mine said . . . it said some pretty mean things."

Suddenly, Stephanie understood. Alexis must have thought that Stephanie, not Jackie, had given her that note.

But how could she think I'd do something like that? Stephanie thought.

"Seems like we have a poison-pen writer on our hands," Coach Becker said. "Did anyone else receive a note?"

Stephanie looked at Jackie again. Jackie's expression reflected pure fear. All Stephanie had to do was tell the coach about the note she got and about Jackie reaching into his bag. She should be thrilled to have this kind of power over Jackie, but something in Jackie's expression made Stephanie almost pity her. She thought about the prayer in her pocket. She could make herself understood right now, but would she herself gain any understanding?

"Well," Coach Becker said, when no one responded, "I'm really disappointed in you all. I thought after today's practice we might have a chance to be a real team. Looks like that's a lost cause." He turned and walked out of the dugout.

Most of the girls rose silently to gather their gear as their parents waited in the parking lot. Stephanie wanted to get away. She wanted to think.

"Stephanie, wait!" she heard Alexis say behind her. She stopped but didn't turn around.

"I know it was you," Alexis said angrily. "You're the one who's been sending those notes."

Stephanie spun around. "Are you crazy?" she asked. "Or just blind? Why would I send notes like that?"

"Because you're jealous of me!" Alexis said.

"What?!"

"Yes, jealous. That's what Jackie says. She says you wanted to pitch and you're mad that I got to. Plus you think you should get to be a model, and you hate me because I am one."

Stephanie glared at Alexis. How could she get it so wrong? *She thinks she's fat when she's way too thin, and now she thinks I was doing everything that Jackie did!*

"Look, Alexis, I promise you I didn't send any of those notes. I saw Jackie putting one into Coach Becker's bag earlier, and I'm pretty sure she wrote the one I found in my bag too."

"You got a note?" Alexis asked in shock.

"Yes, it called me a fat cow. Who knows, maybe you're the one who wrote it. You probably think I'm gigantic." Stephanie was angry at herself for getting so upset, but she couldn't seem to stop herself.

Alexis's eyes grew wet with tears. "I didn't write it. I could never say anything like that to anyone, especially not you. I wish I looked more like you."

Now it was Stephanie's turn to be surprised. "You wish you looked like me?"

"Yeah, I mean, you're so thin and pretty. It really hurt when you kept telling me how thin I was. I figured you were just making fun of me for being fat."

Stephanie shook her head. Alexis had a seriously messed up perception of reality. "I wasn't thinking any of those things, Alexis. Listen, can we just start over and be friends again?"

Alexis looked at her skeptically for a moment and then smiled. "Yeah," she said, "I'd like that." She was quiet for a moment. "Why didn't you tell the coach that you got a note too?"

"I'm not sure. I mean, I wasn't lying to him or anything. It just didn't seem like the right time. I guess I just wanted to give Jackie a chance to tell him herself."

"Not much chance of that," Alexis replied. "Hey, look, there's my mom. I'd better go. She wants us to go work out together this afternoon." And before Stephanie could say anything else, Alexis was gone.

When Stephanie could forget about softball, she really enjoyed her summer vacation. That next week she slept in as late as her mom would allow. She had time to go to all of Todd's therapy sessions. And she spent most afternoons at Aunt Sarah's pool. Matt and Todd even came with her a few times.

She took Carrie's advice and tried to be patient about what she called "the Matt situation." But the more she thought about it, the more she realized she felt more than just friendship for him. Sometimes she got a vibe from him that he felt the same way, but he never said anything.

On Friday evening, just before sunset, as she and Matt walked back from the park where they'd been playing catch, Stephanie had a wild urge to hold his hand. What would he do if she just grabbed it? Would it freak him out and ruin their friendship? She let her hand brush against his a couple of times.

This is so stupid, she thought. *What's wrong with me?*

"Will you come to my game tomorrow?" she asked finally.

"I wouldn't miss it. It sounds better than a soap opera—bitter rivalry, dissension, sickness."

Stephanie laughed and wanted to hold his hand even more. She felt daring, so on impulse she reached for his hand and held on.

He squeezed it softly and then let it go. Her hand

fell to her side. She felt so embarrassed. What must he think of her? The rest of their walk home was silent, and she was barely able to mumble good-bye to him before escaping into the house.

After the hand-holding fiasco, Stephanie regretted inviting Matt to her game. As she and the others warmed up on the field the next afternoon, Matt was all she could think about. If he came, she was afraid she'd be too distracted to play. And if he didn't come . . . well, at least that would tell her how he really felt. But when she saw Alexis, thoughts of Matt immediately flew out of her head.

"Alexis," she said, trying not to look as worried as she felt, "are you feeling OK?"

"I'm fine," Alexis replied. "Just a little nervous."

It was obvious that Alexis didn't want to talk about it, so Stephanie let it drop. "You know you can pitch circles around DeKalb," Stephanie said.

"Thanks, Steph." Alexis smiled weakly. Her skin was pale and blotchy.

Stephanie glanced around to see if she could spot Jackie. The two had not spoken since the last practice, but Stephanie was sure Jackie knew she'd figured out who wrote those notes. *She'd be crazy to try anything now,* Stephanie thought. But she didn't think it would do Alexis any good to have a run-in with Jackie right before the game. It wouldn't do the team any good either. Suddenly, Alexis swayed and almost dropped to her knees.

"You need to sit down," Stephanie said. She dragged Alexis to the dugout and grabbed a sports drink from the cooler. "Now drink this . . . no arguments."

Alexis took a long drink and looked a little better. But Stephanie now knew she had to confront her friend about her condition.

"Look, Alexis, I know you don't want me to say this, but I'm really worried about you. I think you have an eating disorder." Stephanie paused for Alexis's reaction.

To her amazement, Alexis replied, "You're right. I do. You've been right about me the whole time, and I just didn't want to admit it."

"Do your parents know?" Stephanie asked.

"Mom knows I'm trying to lose weight, but she thinks it's a good idea. She's the one who suggested I take laxatives one time before a photo shoot."

Stephanie thought she might vomit. "What about your dad? Have you talked to a doctor?"

"No," Alexis said, "no one else knows."

"Alexis," Stephanie pleaded, "you need help now. Let me tell your dad or Coach Becker."

"Please wait until after the game," Alexis said. "I'll talk to my parents tonight."

"Promise?"

"I promise," Alexis assured her.

Stephanie was still worried about her, but relieved that she'd gotten Alexis to admit she had a problem. Just before the start of the game, she bowed her head and asked God to watch over all of them, especially Alexis.

The Saints started their game against the Corn Huskers in the outfield. Stephanie held down left field with Kelly at third base, Mollie at shortstop, and Amanda in center field. Alexis stood tall and sleek on the pitcher's mound, waiting for the umpire to call the beginning of the game. Stephanie looked at the bleachers and saw Matt take a seat next to her parents. She smiled to herself, but didn't have much time to think about what it meant.

The first batter approached the plate. Stephanie watched as Alexis wound up the ball and pitched. The pitch was not one of her fastest, but it crossed the batter's box without the batter making contact.

"Strike one," the umpire called.

Alexis pitched again. This time the bat made contact with the ball, and it shot out into right field. It was a pop-up that Elise Wagner caught easily. Stephanie relaxed as Alexis wound up for her next pitch.

But instead of throwing the ball, Alexis suddenly collapsed on the pitcher's mound. Stephanie immediately dropped her glove and raced to the mound, along with Coach Becker and Jennifer. Jennifer was calling for help on her cell phone.

"Alexis," Stephanie shouted at the girl who lay unconscious on the ground. Her eyes were shut, and she was not responsive.

"Call an ambulance," Alexis's father shouted as he ran onto the field.

"I did," Jennifer said to him. "Are you her father?"

"Yes, I am," he said. He fell to his knees beside his daughter and called her name. She moved her head slightly and opened droopy eyes. They were glassy.

"Daddy?" she said weakly. "What's wrong?"

"You fainted, sweetheart," he said. Behind him, Alexis's mother peered over his shoulder. She looked terrified. Stephanie felt angry at her, but also felt sorry for her. Whatever lies Alexis had told herself, her mother probably believed them too.

A few minutes later, an ambulance pulled up to the baseball diamond, and two paramedics rushed out with a gurney. They lowered it to ground level and knelt beside Alexis. One of the paramedics checked Alexis's pulse. Stephanie saw him say something to the other paramedic, who was checking her blood pressure. Soon the men carefully lifted Alexis onto the gurney and raised it to load her into the ambulance.

Stephanie and the other girls watched as the ambulance pulled away. Stephanie noticed Jackie reach down and pick something up off the ground and then move away from the rest of the girls. No one spoke to her. Mollie and Elise were both crying, but Stephanie just felt numb. The coaches from both teams made the decision to continue the game.

"She probably just got overheated," Coach Becker told his team. "We'll let you all know as soon as we hear something from the doctors."

Stephanie went back to her position in the outfield and looked toward the pitcher's mound. She was angry—angry at Alexis's mother for putting so much pressure on her. Angry at Jackie for playing mind games with Alexis. And angry at herself that she hadn't gone to the coach with her concerns.

Jackie was now exactly where she most wanted to be—on the pitcher's mound. The Saints were a bit rattled for the next inning or so, but Jackie held the Huskers to three runs, and the Saints, who were playing more like a team than ever, were able to rack up eleven. Stephanie hated to admit it, but Jackie was a terrific pitcher.

If she'd had a better attitude, Stephanie thought, *she probably would have been the starting pitcher all along.*

After the game, the girls gathered in the dugout, hoping to hear some news about Alexis. Even Jackie looked grim. Jennifer finished a conversation on her cell phone and then held a whispered conversation with Coach Becker. Coach left immediately, and Jennifer called for their attention.

"Alexis will be in the hospital for several days," Jennifer said. "Her father has given me permission to tell you what some of you already may have guessed. Alexis suffers from an eating disorder. Her heart has been damaged. The doctors suspect she actually had a minor heart attack during the game, but they expect her to recover. Her parents are looking at treatment options."

Jennifer rubbed her forehead. Seeing her concern for Alexis, Stephanie regretted that she hadn't gotten to know her assistant coach better.

"Ladies," Jennifer continued, "Alexis is probably not the only one of you who will struggle with an eating disorder. I hope what has happened to her will encourage all of you to stay healthy and get help if you need it."

She paused again. "I've heard stories about

softball coaches who pressure the girls on their teams to lose weight so they can run faster. If you ever have a coach who makes you feel bad about your body or encourages you to abuse it, quit. You can't be successful in any sport without taking care of your body."

The girls were quiet as they gathered their gear. Stephanie joined Matt and her parents and told them what Jennifer had said. Stephanie wanted to go to the hospital right away to see Alexis, but her dad said that Alexis might not even have been admitted to a room yet.

"We'll take you tomorrow right after church," he promised.

Her parents gave Matt a ride home, and as she sat in the backseat with him, everything that had happened the night before came rushing back to Stephanie. She hardly said a word to him the whole way home, and he was just as quiet.

"Would you like to come over for some ice cream?" her mom asked him as they entered their neighborhood.

Stephanie held her breath. She wasn't even sure what she wanted him to answer.

"Not tonight, but thanks, Mrs. Swift," he said. "Stephanie's had a hard day. I think I'll just let you guys chill."

Stephanie was both relieved and disappointed. She lay awake a long time that night, wondering how Alexis was doing, and about how she had probably ruined her friendship with Matt.

CHAPTER:08

Stephanie paused outside Alexis's hospital room, said a quick prayer, and crept in. She gasped. Tubes and hoses restricted Alexis to the bed, and bags of fluid hanging on a stainless steel stand dripped slowly into her arm. Wires hooked to her chest connected to a machine monitoring her vital signs.

There was a chair on the other side of the bed against the closed window shade. Alexis was asleep. Stephanie set the vase of flowers she had brought on the small table next to the bed and sat down in the vinyl chair. She reached out and took her sleeping friend's hand. Alexis's eyelids fluttered and opened.

"Hey," Stephanie said softly.

"Hey," Alexis whispered back.

"Go back to sleep," Stephanie suggested. "I'll be here."

Alexis forced a smile. Stephanie was surprised at how pretty her friend's smile was, even with dry, cracked lips. She could see why Alexis was a model. She just couldn't believe that someone would be willing to let a girl starve to get a better photo.

"Can I get you anything?" Stephanie asked.

"Water," Alexis whispered.

Next to the bed on the nightstand was a cup of water with a straw. Stephanie offered it to her friend. Alexis sucked some water into her mouth and then turned her head slightly. Stephanie set the cup back down and reached for her friend's hand again. Alexis tried to squeeze Stephanie's hand, but she had very little strength.

Stephanie sat in the chair as Alexis nodded in and out of consciousness. The room was warm, and Stephanie felt tired. Without meaning to, her eyes closed and she fell asleep with her head on the bed.

She jerked awake when she heard footsteps entering the room. Jackie Wolfe stood just inside the door, holding a colorful basket of summer flowers in one hand and a crumpled paper in the other.

Jackie approached the other side of Alexis's bed and stared down at her. Stephanie could tell that Jackie had been crying.

Without even looking at Stephanie, Jackie asked, "Have you talked to her?"

"She asked me for a drink of water," Stephanie said. "But that's all."

"Will she be OK?" Jackie asked.

"I don't know. I haven't seen her parents."

"They're outside the door," Jackie said. "They told me you were in here with her. They came in earlier and saw you sleeping."

"I wonder if they want to come back in," Stephanie said, rising from the chair.

"No," Jackie said, "they told me we could stay in here with her for a little while."

Alexis opened her eyes again and said, "Stay. Please."

Stephanie and Jackie both nodded. *What a strange little trio we make,* Stephanie thought.

Stephanie gave Alexis another drink of water, and Alexis fell asleep again. Stephanie felt a little trapped. She didn't want to leave, because Alexis had asked her to stay, but she had no idea what to say to Jackie.

"You must hate me," Jackie whispered.

"Hate's a pretty strong word," Stephanie said. She found she didn't have the energy to be angry at Jackie. Besides, it must have taken a lot of courage for Jackie to visit Alexis.

"If you don't, you should," she said. "Look what I found last night. It fell out of Alexis's pocket when she collapsed."

She handed Stephanie the paper in her hand. It was a note written on the same type of paper as the one she'd received. Stephanie flattened it out and read, "'I can't believe a fat cow like you is a model. Maybe if you didn't eat so much, you'd actually be pretty. Or maybe you'll just drop dead.'"

Fury rose up in Stephanie. Alexis had carried this note around with her? The poor girl probably believed every word of it.

"How could you?" Stephanie hissed.

"I don't know!" Jackie said, with tears in her eyes. "I was just jealous of her. But I didn't think she'd believe what I wrote. I mean, she's so thin already. How could she possibly think she was fat? I didn't mean for any of this to happen. It's all my fault!"

Jackie's voice broke on a sob. Stephanie was anxious to calm her down. She didn't want Alexis to wake up right now. The last thing Alexis needed was to talk about that note again.

"This is not all your fault," Stephanie said, suddenly feeling sorry for Jackie. "Alexis had an eating disorder before she joined the team. Your note certainly didn't help, but what happened to Alexis probably would have happened anyway."

"Really?" Jackie sniffed.

"Really," Stephanie said.

"Why are you being so nice to me? I don't deserve it."

"I'm not sure." Stephanie sighed. "Maybe because

I've spent too many angry days in hospital rooms, trying to place blame. Maybe because I think in some ways you're just as messed up and insecure as Alexis. But mostly because I'm a Christian, and Jesus has taught me to love and forgive others, even when it's hard to do."

The two of them talked quietly for the next few minutes. Jackie had a lot of questions about God. They hadn't talked long when Alexis's mom came back in.

"The doctor is coming in to see Alexis now, so could you please excuse us, girls?"

"May I come see her tomorrow?" Stephanie asked.

"Me too?" added Jackie.

"Of course," Mrs. Wilson said. "I'm sure Alexis would love to see her friends again."

Stephanie noticed that Jackie winced a little at the word "friends."

"See you tomorrow then, Mrs. Wilson," Stephanie said, and she and Jackie walked back down the corridor.

On the drive home, Stephanie remembered what her pastor's wife had said about enemies becoming friends. Was it possible for her to become friends with Jackie Wolfe?

The next morning, Jackie was waiting outside the

hospital entrance when Stephanie's mom dropped her off.

"Isn't that the girl from your team who was so awful to everyone?" her mom asked.

Stephanie hadn't felt like explaining to her mom what had happened the day before, so she could understand her mom's surprise.

"Yeah," Stephanie said, "but I think Jackie regrets everything. What happened to Alexis has changed her."

"I can't keep up," her mom said, pushing Stephanie's silky hair out of her face. "Call me when you're done. I've just got a couple of errands to run."

"Hey," Jackie said when Stephanie approached.

"Hey," Stephanie said. "You ready?"

"Ready."

They walked through the lobby and to the elevator, where Jackie pressed the up button. Soon they were standing outside Alexis's room.

"Before we go in there," Jackie said, "I need to say something. I'm really sorry. Not just for what happened to Alexis, but for the way I've acted. I was so angry when I didn't get to pitch that I blamed everyone. I wanted to hurt Alexis and you. But I never wanted anything like this to happen. I'm sorry I wrote you that note, Steph. What I said wasn't true at all. I can't believe how nice you're being to me."

"I can't believe it either," Stephanie said. She was glad they were both able to smile.

When the girls walked into the room, they found Alexis sitting up and watching television, with oxygen tubes in her nose. She looked surprised to see them together, and Stephanie was pretty sure Alexis didn't even remember their visit from the day before.

"Alexis," Jackie said, with tears in her eyes, "I'm sorry about the note. It was stupid and cruel, and I had no idea you were struggling with this."

Alexis was quiet for a long time. At last she said, "Your note just said exactly what I thought about myself."

"How can you think that?" Jackie asked.

"My doctor says it's part of the disease. I don't really understand it all. Looks like I'll get plenty of time to figure it out though. As soon as I'm well enough, I'm going to a treatment center for eating disorders."

"For how long?" Stephanie asked. She hated to think about Alexis's leaving.

"I'm not sure. But don't worry. I hear they're looking for a pitcher for their softball team." Alexis smiled faintly. Stephanie was glad to see she still had a sense of humor.

"Good," Jackie said, "that way you can come back and pitch for the Saints as soon as you're better."

Alexis stared at her. "Thanks for saying that, Jackie," she said. "It means a lot."

"I'm glad you're going to be OK," Stephanie said.

"Me too, I hope," Alexis replied. "Do you think you could pray for me, Stephanie?"

"I'll pray for you every night, Alexis," Stephanie assured her.

"No, Steph, I mean right now." She reached up and held on to both Stephanie and Jackie's hands.

Stephanie's eyes widened. Was it really possible that she was standing next to Alexis's hospital bed in a prayer circle with Jackie Wolfe? She took a deep breath and prayed, "Lord, thank you that Alexis is getting the help she needs. Please teach her to think of herself as you think of her—as your beautiful child. Show Jackie and me how we can help Alexis. And thank you that we can be friends. Lord, we ask this of you in your Son Jesus' name. Amen."

Stephanie opened her eyes to find that Alexis had fallen asleep, and Jackie was staring at her. "Are you really my friend?" Jackie asked.

"Yeah," Stephanie said, "I think so."

"Thanks," Jackie said.

Alexis's dad opened the door.

"Hello, Mr. Wilson," Stephanie whispered.

"Why don't you two come out here," he said. "I'll give you an update on Alexis's condition."

Stephanie gently squeezed Alexis's hand once again before she and Jackie followed him out.

"I guess Alexis probably told you that she's going to a treatment clinic," he said. "It's up in Rockford, but maybe we can work out a way you girls could come up and see her once in a while. She can receive phone calls and e-mails any time."

"We'll definitely keep in touch," Stephanie said.

"Yeah," Jackie said, "you can count on it."

"Thanks for coming to see her," he said. "Stephanie, Alexis told me this morning that you knew something was wrong with her, that you suspected she had an eating disorder."

Stephanie went white. Would he be angry with her for not telling him?

"I just wanted to say thank you," he said, "for being honest with her. You had more courage than I had."

"She's going to be OK, Mr. Wilson," she assured him.

He nodded and entered his daughter's room, and Jackie and Stephanie walked back down the corridor.

"See you at practice?" Stephanie asked when they got to the lobby.

"The jury is still out on that one," Jackie replied.

"What do you mean?" Stephanie said.

"I told Coach Becker about the notes and

everything. He said he wanted some time to think about what to do. He's supposed to call me this afternoon."

"I hope he'll give you another chance," Stephanie said.

"Thanks," said Jackie. "That means a lot."

The next day when Stephanie came downstairs with her towel and swimsuit to go with Todd to hydrotherapy, he looked surprised.

"Didn't I tell you Becky was coming with me today?"

"Have I been replaced by Matt's older sister?" Stephanie asked, trying to sound like she was kidding.

"No, Becky's just been really curious about the therapy. She's thinking about going into that field and asked if she could come along. Of course, it's a plus that she's not hard to look at," he added with a wink. "I'm sorry if I forgot to tell you."

"No problem," Stephanie said, but she felt a little rejected. This was her special time with Todd.

"How's Alexis?" he asked.

"Better," she said. "I talked to her on the phone earlier. She's being transferred to a clinic in Rockford this afternoon."

"And Jackie?"

"I'm not sure if she's still on the team or not. I guess I'll find out tomorrow at practice."

"So, has Francis of Assisi helped you at all?" Todd asked.

Stephanie smiled, thinking about the prayer Todd had shared with her. It gave her an idea. "Yeah," she said, "he's helped a lot."

"Can you find some way to occupy yourself this afternoon without me?" Todd asked.

"Sure," Stephanie said. "I've got a phone call to make anyway."

"To a guy?" he said, teasing her.

"Actually," Stephanie replied, "yes."

When Stephanie arrived at practice the next morning, Jackie was already there.

"So?" Stephanie asked.

"I'm still on the team," Jackie replied, "thanks to you."

"I don't know what you're talking about," Stephanie said innocently.

"Yes, you do. Coach Becker told me you called him and asked him to give me another chance. Thanks."

"Don't thank me," Stephanie said. "Thank Francis of Assisi. He's the one who taught me to be an instrument of peace."

"All right," Jackie said, confused. "Who's Francis and where's Assisi?"

Stephanie laughed. "You'd better warm up that pitching arm," she told Jackie.

"Ladies," Coach Becker said, calling for their attention, "Saturday's game is against the Rochelle Rockets. They only know how to do two things in Rochelle: play softball and watch softball. They'll be a tough team to beat. A few weeks ago, I wouldn't have thought we had a chance. But you girls are full of surprises," he said, looking at Stephanie and Jackie, who were sitting next to each other. "So let's go out and have a great practice."

As they headed out onto the field, Stephanie was surrounded by Elise, Natalie, and Mollie. "So what's up with you and the Queen of Darkness?" Mollie asked, nodding toward Jackie.

"What happened to Alexis really shook up Jackie," Stephanie said. "I think you'll see a big change in her."

It was a great practice. Not only did the girls play well, but they actually had fun, something Stephanie had almost forgotten was possible on the softball field. She felt a little guilty having such a good time while Alexis was in treatment, but she was grateful for the change in the team, and looked forward to telling Alexis.

Only Heather and Amanda seemed a little uncertain. But Stephanie noticed Jackie talking to them during a break, and after that, even they seemed to enjoy themselves.

"If you girls play Saturday like you practiced tonight," Coach Becker said after practice, "we're gonna show those Rockets what fast-pitch is all about. Don't forget to keep Alexis in your thoughts and prayers. See you here Saturday morning."

Stephanie couldn't believe how her life had flip-flopped in the last few days. Everything that had made her miserable—the softball team, Jackie's attitude, her fears for Alexis—seemed to be working out. She e-mailed Alexis every day. Her friend was lonely, but she said everyone was really nice at the clinic, and she knew it was where she needed to be. The doctors were optimistic she'd be home in time to start school that fall.

Stephanie got an e-mail from Jackie too. Jackie was actually smart and funny, when she wasn't bent on ruthlessly destroying the happiness of all those around her.

"Do you think I could go with you to your youth group sometime?" Jackie asked in her e-mail. "My dad has always said church was for losers, and that all they want is to take your money, but you don't seem like that at all."

Stephanie suggested Jackie come with her on Sunday afternoon to youth group. When she logged off, she prayed, "Thank you, God. I'm not sure if I was your 'instrument of peace' or not, but you sure have brought love and peace where there had been hatred!"

Those were the good things. But at home she felt lonely. Todd was spending more and more time with Becky. Stephanie wanted to be happy for him, and she really liked Becky, but she missed the time with her older brother. The worst part was that even though Becky was around all the time, Matt wasn't coming over at all. She hadn't had a real conversation with him since the night she'd tried to hold his hand. Even thinking about that now filled her with regret. How could she have been so stupid?

He's probably just avoiding me so he doesn't have to tell me he's not interested, she thought.

On Friday night, Todd went out with Becky, and her parents asked her to play cards with them.

"It's not the most exciting way to spend a Friday night," her mom said, "but I'll make popcorn. You could ask Matt over to play with us if you want."

"No thanks, Mom," Stephanie said. "I think I'll just grab a book and read for a while." She hadn't told her mom anything that was going on with Matt. Stephanie avoided making eye contact and went to her room. A few minutes later, her cell phone rang. It was Matt.

"Want to go for a walk?" he asked. "I'd like to talk to you about some things. I could be there in about half an hour."

"Sure," Stephanie said, feeling really nervous. "See you then."

Stephanie spent the time trying on every outfit in her closet. She wanted to look nice, but not like she was trying too hard or anything. What did he want to talk about? Finally, she ran downstairs.

"Mom, is it OK if Matt and I take a walk?"

"Sure," she said, "but be home by nine-thirty."

Stephanie waited on the front porch. She thought Matt looked really nice when she saw him coming up her sidewalk. Instead of his usual T-shirt and baggy shorts, he was dressed in khaki pants and a blue button-down shirt. She was glad she'd put on her jean skirt instead of her soccer shorts.

"Want to get some ice cream?" he said. "Louders is open later now for summer."

"Sure," Stephanie said. They walked in silence for the three blocks to the little family-owned ice cream stand. The place was packed.

"Why don't you go find a bench or something for us?" Matt suggested. "I'll get the ice cream. Do you want your usual?"

"Butterfinger flurry with whipped cream," she confirmed.

"What else?" he asked, smiling, and got in line.

There were no seats anywhere around Louders, but she noticed that the park across the street had a few empty benches. She waved at Matt and pointed so he'd know where to find her, and then she found a bench next to the pond. She hoped the geese wouldn't bug them too much, but they were at the other end of the pond where some kids were throwing bread to them.

Finally Matt got through the line and found her. "Here you go," he said.

She started to pull a few dollars out of your purse. "Don't worry about it," he said. "My treat."

They lapsed back into silence, and Stephanie was afraid that the two of them were going to remain speechless the entire evening. Matt finally broke the silence.

"So, do you know what classes you're taking in school this fall?"

"No," she said, "we're meeting with a guidance counselor in a few weeks to figure it out."

"You think you'll be taking any history classes?"

"Probably," she said.

"Does that mean you've gotten over your hatred of dates?"

"What?" she asked.

"It's just that you told me that you hated dates,

but I was kind of hoping that . . . well, you had different feelings about different kinds of dates," he said, steadily looking at his shoes. "For example, you might hate a date like 1066, when the Normans won the Battle of Hastings in Britain—"

"How do you remember that?" she began, but he interrupted.

"But a date like 1492, that one's pretty easy to remember, because it rhymes with 'ocean blue,'" he said.

"Matt," she said, "what are you talking about?"

"It's like this," he said. "I'm sorry I freaked out a little the other day when you . . . held my hand."

Stephanie felt her face grow hot. "I don't want to talk about it."

"But I do," he said, and caught her by the hand. "It scared me because our friendship means so much to me. I don't want to make things weird by being more than friends."

Stephanie's heart was beating wildly, but she felt a little angry. "Oh," she said, "I'm sorry to make things weird for you."

"Well, they are weird."

"Why?" she said. "Why can't we just forget about what happened and go back to being friends?"

"No," Matt said, "I don't think I can do that."

Stephanie freed her hand and ran away from him,

past the pond, scattering geese in her path. She could hear his footsteps behind her.

"Steph," he said, catching her, "please." She stopped but didn't turn around. "Things are weird in our friendship because now when I'm not with you all I think about is you, and when I'm with you all I can do is think about how to be closer to you," he said a little breathlessly. Stephanie turned around. "I don't want to lose your friendship, Steph, but do you think you could get over your hatred of dates enough to consider this our first one?"

The corners of Stephanie's mouth twitched. "I'm not allowed to go on dates with a boyfriend until I'm sixteen," she said.

"What about with a boy who is already a friend?"

"If we're always in a group, I think it's OK."

"Do geese count?" Matt asked. They laughed and returned to the bench.

The morning sun bore down on the softball field, but a cool breeze from the north made the late June day more bearable. Jackie stood on the pitcher's mound, warmed up and ready. Natalie Hillshire was dressed in her catcher's gear and practicing with Jackie. Stephanie, Mollie, and Elise threw a ball back and forth in the outfield, while Jenny, Amanda, and Kelly covered the bases, throwing fastballs to each other. Heather took up her position as shortstop.

Stephanie scanned the bleachers for her parents. They were there, and Todd had come too, along with Becky and Matt. Matt waved at her, and she grinned.

"Is that your boyfriend?" Heather asked.

Stephanie almost laughed. It was funny to think of Matt that way. "Yeah, he is."

"Cute!" Heather replied.

Coach Becker called the girls to the dugout. But to Stephanie's surprise, Jennifer, not Coach Becker, addressed the team.

"Ladies," she said, "you look great out there, because you're playing as a team. So go out there and win this one for Alexis."

The teams were introduced, and the Saints ran back onto the field. Jackie and Natalie exchanged a couple of last-minute power pitches. Stephanie thought the team looked ready to win, and she could see some of the girls on the Rockets whispering to each other. Probably nothing they had heard about this year's Chapel Hill Saints had prepared them for the team they were actually facing.

The first Rocket on deck gripped her bat as Jackie rocked back and forth on the pitcher's mound, waiting for the umpire to start the game.

"Play ball!" he shouted.

Jackie cocked her arm and twirled backward, pitching as if she were bowling for a strike. The ball shot across the plate and into Natalie's waiting glove.

"Strike one!" shouted the umpire.

Stephanie thought a few minutes later the umpire might be tired of calling strikes, because that was all Jackie pitched. Three up and three down for the Rockets, all strikeouts, and it was the bottom of the first.

The game was scoreless until the bottom of the fourth. Stephanie stepped up to bat. The Saints bases were loaded. As she stood in the batter's box, Jackie told her, "Hit it like you did against me last time!" Stephanie thought about her home run. She'd been angry then. Could she do it again?

She could and did. Suddenly, the score was 4–0 Saints, and the crowd was going crazy. Stephanie could hear Matt and her mom yelling louder than anyone. Elise ended the sixth inning with a run, and Jackie prepared for the top of the seventh.

"You can do it," Stephanie whispered to her. Jackie was poised to pitch another no-hitter—her first in the ponytail league.

Jackie wound up for the first pitch of the inning. The batter played it safe, swinging at only perfect balls. Three strikes later, she walked back to the bench. The second batter came out confidently, but the girl was no match for Jackie's change-ups. A fast pitch a little to the batter's right threw the girl off because the one before was pitched further out to the left. The second batter was out in three swings.

Stephanie could see Jackie and Natalie staring hard at each other. She was amazed by the way Natalie was able to sense the direction of Jackie's pitches.

"Strike one!" the umpire called as the batter came out of her swing to see the ball resting comfortably in Natalie's glove.

The batter prepared for the next pitch. Jackie's hip pivoted as she released the pitch. It appeared to be slightly outside, and the batter didn't swing. But Natalie didn't even have to reach out to catch the ball.

"Strike two!"

This was it. Jackie looked nervous on the pitcher's mound, but one good pitch and the game would be over.

"You can do this, Jackie," Stephanie yelled. "Come on, Jackie." Around her in the dugout, the rest of the team joined her in chanting Jackie's name. Soon the crowd joined in, but then hushed as Jackie braced herself for the pitch.

Jackie sent the ball sailing. The batter panicked

and took a swing, but the ball was low. Natalie caught it with ease.

"Strike three!" the umpire said. Most of the crowd had said it with him. The Saints ran to the field and piled around Jackie.

"That was awesome!" Stephanie said as soon as she got close enough.

"Thanks," Jackie said. "I did it for Alexis . . . and for the team."

Check out other books in this series . . .

GAME ON!

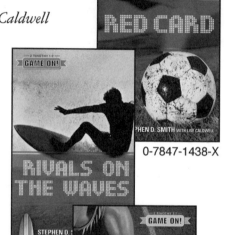

Stephen D. Smith with Lise Caldwell

GAME ON! is a sports fiction series featuring young athletes who must overcome obstacles—on and off the field. The characters in these stories are neither the best athletes nor the underdogs. These are ordinary kids of today's culture—characters you'll identify with and be inspired by.

RED CARD

0-7847-1438-X

RIVALS ON THE WAVES

0-7847-1470-3

HIGH HURDLES

0-7847-1439-8

FOURTH AND LONG

0-7847-1471-1

www.standardpub.com
or
1-800-543-1353